FALLING FOR HER IMPOSSIBLE BOSS

BY
ALISON ROBERTS

MILLS
BOON

First published in Great Britain 2012
by Mills & Boon, an imprint of Harlequin (UK) Limited,
Eton House, 18-24 Paradise Road, Richmond, Surrey TW9 1SR

© Allison Roberts 2012

ISBN: 978 0 263 22880 9

Heartbreakers of St Patrick's Hospital

The delicious doctors
you know you *shouldn't* fall for!

St Patrick's Hospital: renowned for
cutting-edge lifesaving procedures…
and Auckland's most sinfully sexy surgeons—
there's never a shortage of female patients
in this waiting room!

The hospital grapevine buzzes with
rumours about motorbike-riding rebel
doc Connor Matthews and aristocratic
neurosurgeon Oliver Dawson—
but one thing's for sure… They're the
heartbreakers of St Patrick's and
should be firmly off limits.…

**So why does that make them
even more devastatingly attractive?!**

Also available this month from
Mills & Boon® Medical™ Romance:

Book 1 in
Heartbreakers of St Patrick's Hospital

THE LEGENDARY PLAYBOY SURGEON

Alison Roberts lives in Christchurch, New Zealand, and has written over sixty Mills & Boon® Medical Romances. As a qualified paramedic, she has personal experience of the drama and emotion to be found in the world of medical professionals, and loves to weave stories with this rich background—especially when they can have a happy ending.

When Alison is not writing, you'll find her indulging her passion for dancing or spending time with her friends (including Molly the dog) and her daughter Becky, who has grown up to become a brilliant artist. She also loves to travel, hates housework, and considers it a triumph when the flowers outnumber the weeds in her garden.

Recent titles by the same author:

SYDNEY HARBOUR HOSPITAL: ZOE'S BABY**
THE HONOURABLE MAVERICK
THE UNSUNG HERO
ST PIRAN'S: THE BROODING HEART SURGEON†
THE MARRY-ME WISH*
WISHING FOR A MIRACLE*
NURSE, NANNY…BRIDE!

***Sydney Harbour Hospital*
*Part of the *Baby Gift* collection
†*St Piran's Hospital*

These books are also available in eBook format from www.millsandboon.co.uk

CHAPTER ONE

'OH, NO…it's *you*, isn't it?'

Was that appalled-sounding male voice referring to her? Annabelle Graham turned her head just far enough to see the speaker and her heart sank like a stone. Later, she would realise she'd known who it was even before she turned her head. Those clipped private school kind of vowels that, for her at least, totally obliterated the sexiness such a deep voice should automatically have.

She would also realise that such an outburst was completely out of character so he must have been even more appalled to see her than his tone had suggested. Bella sucked in a long breath that she knew would get expelled in a resigned sigh as she turned her head far enough to be polite.

Oliver Dawson, eminent neurosurgeon here at St Patrick's hospital, looked like he'd frozen in mid-step as he'd been passing by the dayroom of this ward. He almost looked as if he'd been hit by a bolt of lightning. Her breath came out in the anticipated sigh.

One of the only immediately discernible perks of finishing her run in Theatre and starting her new nursing rotation in the geriatric wards had been the thought of not looking like an idiot in front of this man again.

Bumping into things. Not wearing her mask properly. Not being in the right place at the right time.

Just not being…good enough. At anything.

It should have occurred to her that he might have patients in this area of the hospital. Old people had strokes. They got brain tumours. They fell over and suffered head injuries. Bella's heart sank even further. This was probably one of Mr Dawson's most frequent ports of call now that she came to think about it.

And, yep, she was the 'you' he had to be referring to because he had her pinned with a glare that was in no way softened by the rich chocolate shade of his eyes. And heaven help her, he was even more intimidating in a three-piece pinstriped suit than he had been in loose-fitting theatre scrubs.

The appalled tone was distressingly familiar. Being bailed up to get told off was not a new experience by any means. Bella sighed again.

'Yes,' she confessed. 'It's me.' She tried a bright smile. 'How are you, Mr Dawson?'

The glare took on an incredulous tinge but Bella was distracted by realising that this was the first time she had seen the surgeon without his hair being covered by a theatre cap. It was even darker than his eyes and as immaculately cut as his suit. There was an air of precision and control about Oliver Dawson that was undoubtedly a huge asset as a surgeon but he was on another planet as far as the men Bella had ever tried to placate. The smile seemed to hit some kind of force-field and bounce straight back at her. Oliver not only ignored her polite enquiry about his wellbeing, he was looking past her now.

'*What* are you doing here?'

'I've just started my rotation on Geriatrics.' Bella's first run in St Patrick's had been in Theatre. After her three-month stint in the dreaded area of the elderly and infirm, she had Paediatrics to look forward to—her all-time favourite. It was going to be a few years until she could start a family of her own so Bella had every intention of making the most of being with other people's children until then. Her next run couldn't come soon enough. Especially now. But neurosurgical cases were fairly common with children, too, weren't they? Where would she be safe from failing to make the grade in Oliver Dawson's eyes? Did they need a nurse in Dermatology Outpatients, perhaps? Obs and Gynae?

A single, curt shake of the man's head told her that her response to his question had been incorrect. Well, no surprises there.

'I wasn't referring to the details of your employment roster,' he snapped. 'I would like to know what you are doing right now. With these patients.'

'Oh…' Bella turned back to find herself being watched with some sympathy by five pairs of eyes, most of which were behind fairly thick spectacle lenses. It was only then that Bella became aware again of the music coming from the cute little speaker she'd attached to her iPod. Good ol' foot-stomping country music. She could understand that it would seem a little inappropriate. And loud.

'I'll turn it down,' she offered hurriedly, following the words with action. 'I had to turn it up because Wally's pretty deaf and he couldn't hear the beat.'

'Aye.' The rotund, elderly man standing closest to Bella nodded vigorously. 'Deaf as a doorknob, I am.'

Wally got ignored, something that was rude enough to irritate Bella enormously. Typical surgeon, thinking he was God's gift and so important that he didn't have to observe common courtesy. When he also ignored the other four elderly people standing in silence, looking decidedly nervous as the consultant in the suit flicked his glance across the whole line, her irritation mounted to active dislike. Maybe this man had become a surgeon because he preferred to deal with people who were unconscious. Maybe he didn't really give a damn about how small he was making anybody here feel.

The raking glance finished with Bella.

'You haven't answered my question.'

He was speaking slowly, with a tone that suggested her intellect was sadly below par. A bit like the way he'd told her she should be in a nursery if she was going to wear her surgical mask like a bib.

Dislike was firmly established now. Old. Rebellion bloomed.

'We're having a line-dancing class,' she informed Oliver Dawson crisply. 'To be precise, we're learning The Electric Slide.' She smiled at the inpatients she'd found looking so incredibly bored in the dayroom of this ward when she'd started working here last week.

It wasn't as though she was forcing them to do something they didn't want to do and she wasn't supposed to be doing anything else herself. She was on her break, for heaven's sake. She wasn't doing anything wrong and they'd all been having fun until this pompous surgical consultant had interrupted them. Now she might

have trouble persuading any of these oldies to get out of
their chairs again judging by how confused poor Edna
was looking. By the time Wally had looked from Bella
to Mr Dawson and back again, he was huffing indig-
nantly. He'd probably need his inhaler very soon. She
smiled at them all reassuringly.

'We were getting pretty good at it, too, weren't we?
Let's leave it for now and we'll have another go tomorrow. I'll bet we can get that stomp and clap on four
sorted by then.'

Verity, who'd been bravely attempting line dancing
with the aid of her walking frame, was the only one
who smiled back.

'That will be lovely, dear. Remember not to come and
get me until after I've fed the hens, though.'

Oliver shook his head with disbelief, turning away as
he saw the nurse starting to assist her patients back to
their chairs in front of the television soap opera running
in the corner of the dayroom. He even heard her start to
discuss the merits of different types of hen food with
the confused old woman after telling the overweight
gentleman to have a look in his dressing-gown pocket
for his inhaler.

Line dancing? With frail, elderly patients who were
at enough risk of falling and injuring themselves just
getting through the activities of daily life?

Ridiculous. Irresponsible and…and airheaded. About
what he would have expected from the nurse whose
name he didn't even know.

He'd remembered her, though, hadn't he? Even in
theatre scrubs she'd been distracting, with those un-

usually dark blue eyes and the wispy blonde curls that seemed incapable of accepting complete restraint within the confines of an elasticised theatre cap. She had a mouth that seemed permanently on the verge of laughter, too. Inappropriate in the serious environment of an operating theatre and he'd certainly noticed that when she'd had the nerve to wander into *his* theatre with her mask dangling around her neck like a damn bib.

Oliver stalked past the nurses' station on his way up the back stretch of the U-shaped ward. He caught sight of another nurse's uniform behind the counter.

'Sally?'

The charge nurse looking up from the computer screen. 'Oliver! You're early for a visit today.'

'I had an empty slot in my outpatient clinic so I thought I'd pop up.' He cleared his throat. 'Have you got any idea what's going on in your dayroom?'

Sally grinned. 'The line-dancing class?'

Oliver didn't return the smile. 'Yes.'

'It's great, isn't it? She's only been here for a few days but I've never seen anyone establish a rapport with patients quite the way she has.'

'I can imagine.'

Sally didn't seem to notice the dryness of his comment.

'She's getting people moving more than any of the physios or occupational therapists have simply because she's making it so much fun. Daniel told me today that he's thinking of incorporating line dancing into his future physiotherapy routines. He's never thought of it before because he works with people individually. Diversional therapy for whole groups is something we associate with rest homes, not hospitals.' Sally shook her head. 'Who'd have thought? A junior nurse could be starting a revolution.'

Oliver pressed his lips together. There wasn't much point in making his disapproval known if the physiotherapists and other professionals were happy about this. Would he have to wait until of the patients tripped over and broke a wrist or worse before he could step in and make sure the plug got pulled on this unconventional and very dubious activity?

Frustration bubbled. It wasn't even his call really, was it? He could, of course, have a word with his senior colleagues in Geriatrics. Yes…that was the way to go. He didn't usually tap into the influence he had always been able to exert but maybe this was a case of having to override the professional with a more personal status. The thought should have been satisfying but, instead, it led to a very disturbing thought. The muscles around his lips strengthened their hold.

'Lady Dorothy?' The query was succinct. Surely his mother wouldn't have been tempted to not only make a fool of herself but endanger her fragile health by co-operating with the blonde bimbo nurse and her outrageous activities?

Sally's face softened. 'She's in her room,' she said quietly. 'I'm sorry, Oliver, but she's still refusing to try anything in the way of rehab or social activities.'

With a nod, Oliver was on his way to the private room at the end of the corridor. Refusing to participate in social activities in an environment like this was perfectly understandable but some form of rehab was essential if his mother wasn't going to lose an enormous amount of quality of life. He paused for a moment in front of the closed door of the private room and the curtains on the corridor side windows were pulled shut. How many people would be walking past without even realising that one of most revered society matrons in Auckland was an inpatient of St Patrick's?

Lady Dorothy Dawson was in bed. She was resting against a mound of pillows with a silk shawl around her shoulders and the silver waves of her hair brushed and shining but she looked pale and unhappy. Her face brightened as Oliver moved to her bedside.

'Oliver! What a lovely surprise!'

Kissing the soft skin of his mother's cheek, Oliver realised that part of her pallor was due to the fact that Lady Dorothy was not wearing any make-up. She'd probably allowed a nurse to brush her hair but to let a stranger do something more personal like applying foundation or lipstick would be galling, wouldn't it? Especially to a woman who'd always been as proud and independent as his mother.

'How are you, Mother?'

'I'm fine, darling. I'd like to go home.'

'Soon.' His smile hid an increasing anxiety as Oliver took a seemingly casual glance around the room. He was becoming very good at assimilating the information he needed at lightning speed.

The joints in his mother's hands were still swollen and angry from the vicious recurrence of her arthritis. She looked as if she was still losing weight, probably because she was refusing to allow anyone, even him, to help her eat and for days now her only intake had been smoothies or cool soups that she could sip through a straw. The weight loss wasn't the main worry, however. The combination of reduced food intake and her illness was playing havoc with her blood-sugar levels, making control of her insulin-dependent diabetes very difficult.

'How's the pain?'

Lady Dorothy simply gave him a look and Oliver had to smile. It was exactly the kind of look he remembered from when he'd been a small child and he'd hurt himself in some fashion. The 'suck it up and get on with it' look because pain was an inconvenience that couldn't be allowed to interfere with life being lived. Or duty being done. It was the way Lady Dorothy had been raised and the way she'd raised her only son.

His mother might look like an ultimately pampered member of the most elite social circle to be found in the young country of New Zealand but he knew she had the strength of a tiger and a heart of purest gold. Her fundraising efforts were legendary and St Patrick's had benefited along with countless other institutions and charitable organisations. Lady Dorothy was seventy-three years old and had never needed to work for financial reasons but she put more time and effort into her passion than some forty-year-old CEOs of large corporations ever did.

If being able to be hands on for her work had come to an end, Lady Dorothy would be devastated but right now she wouldn't be able to make a phone call, let alone hold a pen. And if her blood-sugar levels couldn't be stabilised she wouldn't be able to drive her car or be left alone at any time due to the risk of her falling into a diabetic coma. While she'd always had help running their enormous property with the help of a housekeeper and gardener, more intrusive staff had always been spurned. An invasion of privacy that simply wasn't acceptable.

Changes were coming, that was for sure. For both of them. Oliver could also be sure that his mother would fight them every step of the way. Achieving them would be no kind of victory either. Not when each one would be so painful for her to accept, removing more and more of her independence and dignity.

He summoned a smile for his mother. 'It's a glorious day. If you got dressed, I might be able to take you for a ride in a wheelchair when I've finished work. It would do you good to get a breath of fresh air.'

His mother shook her head. He clearly needed to find more of an incentive than fresh air. And quickly. A glance at his watch told him he was running out of time and his registrar would be looking for him in Outpatients.

'We could even find something nice for your dinner.' He raised an eyebrow. 'I happen to know where a fast-food joint is.' His smile broadened as he took out the big guns and tapped into his mother's most secret vice. 'Cheeseburgers,' he suggested. 'And French fries.'

The idea was brilliant. Even with her fingers so stiff and useless, Lady Dorothy might be able to manage that kind of food and it would pack enough calories for even a small amount to be helpful. To his horror, however, his mother's eyes shone with sudden tears. They were gone by the time she had shaken her head in a negative response but Oliver could feel her anguish. He touched her hand gently.

'What's wrong, Mum?'

'Sophie,' his mother said, her voice wobbling.

'Who's Sophie?'

Was that the name of the clumsy, line-dancing blonde who was masquerading as a nurse? If she'd done something to upset his mother this much then she wouldn't know what hit her. It occurred to him that defending his mother so vigorously in public might brand him as some kind of mummy's boy, but there was no way he wouldn't protect his mother with everything he had. She was the only family he had. The only person that really mattered in his world, come to that. And did he care what a junior nurse with oversized blue eyes thought of him?

Of course he didn't. The idea was laughable.

'She's the occupational therapist,' Lady Dorothy told him. 'She came in this morning with the kind of clothes she said were ideal because I'd be able to learn to get dressed by myself.'

'Oh?' Oliver was assimilating more than the information. Was he relieved that this Sophie wasn't the nurse and he wouldn't have to verbally rip her to shreds and watch those ready-to-laugh lips wobble when she began to cry?

That he wouldn't be in danger of revealing something as personal and vaguely shameful as the fact that he was a thirty-six-year-old man who still lived with his mother? Well, it could hardly be considered living with his mother when they both had entirely separate wings of the house but he was still living at home, wasn't he?

And why was he even thinking about how that might appear to some nurse whose name he didn't even know? It was bizarre.

'They were…track pants, Oliver. With…an elasticised waist.'

'Oh...'

Track pants. A kind of symbol that his mother equated with fluffy slippers, going out with a chiffon scarf covering hair curlers and a cigarette dangling from a mouth corner. It wasn't that his mother was a snob—she had genuine friends from all walks of life—but self-discipline was everything and meeting personal standards was a matter of pride. Wearing track pants would be as degrading as putting Lady Dorothy into a nappy.

Something had to be done. But what? This was new territory for both Oliver and his mother. He needed to think. In the meantime, he needed to find a way of helping his mother cope somehow.

'How 'bout I bring the burgers and fries in here? Disguised in a plain brown paper bag?' An old joke for a treat that was deemed illicit.

The flicker of amusement was only for his benefit. 'Thanks, darling, but don't go to any trouble. I don't expect I'll be very hungry.' She had turned her head away very slightly. 'It really is time we stopped that ridiculously unhealthy habit, don't you think?'

Oliver was taken aback by the strong realisation that he didn't agree with his mother's suggestion.

The disturbing awareness that something was happening that might prove to be beyond his control was less than pleasant.

The occasional foray into the dark side of healthy eating was hardly a habit for either of them. It was a once-in-a-blue-moon kind of thing, in fact, but it had been a part of their lives for a long, long time. So long that it had become one of his earliest memories. A rare, *good* memory. One that had bestowed a little pleasure in a life that had often been less than joyful for both himself and his mother.

OK, maybe it was an ancient ritual associated with childhood and no longer of any significance but losing it would be...

As sad as seeing his mother like this?

He heard Lady Dorothy's intake of breath. A determined, suck-it-up kind of breath.

'Don't let me take up too much of your time, Oliver. I'm sure you must have far more important things to be doing.'

'I've got a clinic to finish, that's all.' Oliver could feel his frown steadily deepening. There had to be a way through this. 'And then a theatre slot this afternoon. And you have to eat, you know that. I'll be back later.'

With French fries, at least. He wasn't ready to let go of the past to that extent. He didn't think his mother was either. This was just a sign of how miserable she was feeling right now. With a bit of time, she might get over the upsetting episode of the track pants.

Coming back later was a good idea in more ways than one. If that extraordinarily annoying and probably incompetent nurse was on duty now, she would be due to finish her shift by three p.m.

There was no chance she would be anywhere in the vicinity if he slipped in quietly this evening with some fast food to try and tempt his mother's appetite and that suited Oliver very well.

Very well indeed.

CHAPTER TWO

'LADY who?'

Bella was somewhat distracted from what Sally was telling her because she'd spotted Oliver Dawson leaving the ward. He wore the suit very well, she had to admit albeit grudgingly. If only he was a bit…nicer, she would go as far as thinking he was very good looking. OK, gorgeous, then.

'Lady Dorothy,' Sally said.

'Doesn't she have a last name?'

'Of course she does, but nobody uses it. And she's a very well-known personality who doesn't want her admission to hospital being broadcast so it's important that you're discreet.' Sally frowned at Bella. 'Can you be discreet?'

'Of course I can.' Bella straightened her back. She was being given a new responsibility here. Never mind that it probably had something to do with the ward being even more short-staffed than usual. Bella wanted to prove herself. Partly because she was finding the work here far more enjoyable than she had anticipated but it was also the sight of Oliver Dawson's retreating back that was firing her new ambition.

She *was* good at her job. Maybe now people around here would have the chance to find that out.

'What do you want me to do?'

'She's due for a BGL test. We'll hold off on her insulin until I've talked to her doctor. That's more of an excuse to get you into her room, though.' Sally hesitated for a moment and then spoke quietly. 'Lady Dorothy's pretty down at the moment and nobody has been able to get her motivated about the rehab she needs to get started on urgently.' The charge nurse gave her new recruit a thoughtful glance. 'You might be just the person to manage it. I mean, anyone that can get Wally up and dancing has got to have an approach that's drastically different. Just…tread carefully, OK?'

With that rather odd warning echoing in her head, Bella set off for the private room she'd been curious about ever since she'd arrived. The closed door and curtains had fuelled her overactive imagination and she'd decided there was somebody in the room who had some terrible disfigurement they didn't want anybody to see. She'd told her Aunt Kate that she thought it was probably the hunchback of Notre Dame in there.

It was a bit of a disappointment to find it was an elderly woman. An extraordinarily beautiful woman, in fact, with skin that looked like it belonged on a peach and the most amazing silver hair Bella had ever seen. She kept stealing glances as she went through the routine of finger pricking and collecting a drop of blood to put on the end of the testing strip that was fitted into the glucometer. She did the job as gently as possible. Poor Lady Dorothy had a very nasty case of arthritis affecting both hands. Her joints were red and swollen and it looked as though she couldn't move her fingers at all.

Her patient wasn't talking either. As the glances added up, Bella could see the sadness and her heart went out to the old lady. A real lady, no less.

'Why do you keep looking at me like that?'

Bella jumped. 'Sorry, was I being rude? It's just that I *love* your hair. If you could bottle a colour like that, you could make a fortune.'

'It's just grey.'

'Oh, no...' Bella shook her head emphatically. 'It's pure silver. And it sparkles. I had a pair of Lycra dance tights that were just that colour. I loved them, too.'

But Lady Dorothy had lapsed back into silence. She was just sitting there, against her pillows, staring into space. Bella moved around the room, tidying things here and there. Heavens, it was hardly going to impress Sally if she didn't get anything more than a disparaging comment about hair colour as a response when she was supposed to be cheering this patient up.

The huge vase of fresh flowers probably needed some water but when Bella walked towards them, she caught her foot on a chair leg and sent something flying.

Thank goodness Mr Dawson wasn't around to witness her clumsiness. She could almost hear his voice saying something scathing like how typical of her that was.

With an exasperated huff, Bella reached down to scoop up the bright pink object. Why on earth should she even care what he thought of her anyway? She wasn't going to go back to being a theatre nurse. He'd put her off for life.

The huff became a gasp as she realised what she was holding.

'Oh, my God!' She held up the thick, fleecy track pants with the wide elasticised waistband and viewed the item of clothing with horror. And then she felt her cheeks getting hot and whirled around to face the woman in the bed. 'I do apologise, Lady Dorothy,' she said. 'These must be yours.'

The look she got was pure ice. 'They most certainly are *not* mine.'

'Oh…thank God for that.'

Lady Dorothy was still glaring at her. Bella tried a tentative smile.

'I shouldn't say that because it's no joke that my grandfather murdered my grandmother, but you know what?'

Lady Dorothy continued to stare but her eyebrows were moving slowly. In an upward direction. 'What?' The query was understandably wary.

Bella lowered her voice to a confidential tone. 'If she'd been wearing pink track pants like this it could well have been a motive.' Her lips twitched. 'If I'd been on the jury and these were exhibit A then I'd certainly consider them to be an exonerating factor.'

Finally, there was a response from the elderly lady. A lip twitch that mirrored Bella's. She unceremoniously rolled up the offending pants and put them back on the chair.

'So, if they're not yours, what are they doing in here? Shall I get rid of them for you?'

'Best not, dear.'

'How come?'

Lady Dorothy's sigh was weary. 'The occupational therapist brought them. I'm supposed to wear them because I'll be able to put them on by myself.'

'What? Is she trying to drive you to drink or something? What's wrong with the kind of pants you usually wear? Oh…' Bella grimaced. 'Sorry, I'm putting my foot in it again. You probably don't wear trousers at all. I'd imagine you wearing beautiful skirts and jackets or elegant dresses.'

'I do wear trousers. I was wearing my favourite pair when I came in here. They're hanging in the wardrobe.'

Bella opened the small closet. A pair of crisply pressed, pale grey linen pants could be seen. She lifted out the hanger and eyed the garment. 'You know, I'm no expert but the only problem I can see with these is the zip and buttons and that could be easily fixed with an invisible strip of Velcro.'

Lady Dorothy was watching her closely now. 'What about pulling them up?'

'You could use one of those stick gripper things. Has the occupational therapist shown you all the aids you can get now?'

'She showed me a lot of things.' Lady Dorothy's tone suggested she hadn't been impressed.

'Anyway,' Bella added cautiously, 'you'll probably get a lot of movement back when the inflammation goes down. As long as you're not as silly as my nanna was, that is.'

Lady Dorothy blinked. 'What's your nanna got to do with this? I thought you said she got murdered.'

'That was Grandma. On my dad's side and I never knew her. She was the skeleton in my family closet.

Nanna was Mum's mother and she lived with us for a while when she couldn't manage any more. I loved her to bits.'

'You said she was silly.'

Bella nodded, happy to finally have the old lady's full attention. She wasn't even looking sad any more. 'She had a high horse. We used to tease her about getting on it so often.'

'I don't understand.'

'She was very critical of people she didn't like—especially doctors. She didn't believe in drugs of any kind. When she was diagnosed with her rheumatoid arthritis her GP told her to get off her high horse for once and do as she was told because if she didn't take the painkillers and anti-inflammatories and do her exercises, she'd end up totally crippled by the disease.'

'And did she?'

'No. She went home and flushed all the pills down the loo and, of course, she couldn't keep moving because her joints were all too swollen and sore and she did end up crippled and had to come and live with us.' Bella sighed. 'I wish she'd been put somewhere like here when she got sick. She would have loved my line-dancing classes. *That* would have got her moving.'

There was a sparkle in Lady Dorothy's eyes now. A look of real interest. Determination, even? 'What on earth is line dancing?'

Bella's grin was mischievous. 'I'll come and get you tomorrow and you can find out.'

'Oh, I couldn't do that.'

'Why not?'

'I wouldn't be dressed for it.'

It was Bella's turn to raise her eyebrows significantly. 'But you've got your clothes right there in the wardrobe. I'm not asking you to wear shocking pink trackie daks. In fact,' she put on a stern face. 'I'm quite sure they not allowed for line dancing.'

'But...'

Bella could see a fear she could understand in this beautiful woman's face. The fear of loss of dignity. Of losing herself in her disease. Without thinking, she went and perched her hip on the side of the bed and took one of Lady Dorothy's hands in her own.

'I do understand,' she said softly. 'I had to help my nanna with things that were just plain embarrassing for both of us until we got used to it but I learned something. Something important.'

She could see the effort it took Lady Dorothy to swallow and then speak. Her voice was a whisper. 'What was that?'

'That the physical stuff like being able to get dressed or even go to the loo by yourself—it's all on the outside. If you can get past the inconvenience of needing help it doesn't change a thing that really matters—the person you are on the inside.'

There was a long moment of silence. Bella shut her eyes for a moment to gather her courage.

'We could have a go with your clothes now, if you like. That way we could find out what needs a bit of adjustment in the way of fastenings and things.'

More silence. It was obvious that some time was needed. 'Have a think about it, anyway,' Bella suggested. 'In the meantime, I could tell you about something really funny that my kitten did this morning. Do you like cats?'

'I used to.' The tone was wistful. 'I haven't had a pet for many years.'

Bella smiled. 'Well…I live with my aunt Kate who's very particular about stuff and Bib—that's the kitten—decided she wanted to see what was on top of the window and the quickest way up was to use the net curtains, only her claws got stuck and she got scared and started shouting.' Bella was using her hands as she began her story but Lady Dorothy wasn't watching. Her gaze kept straying to the wardrobe door that Bella had left open accidentally. The linen pants were in clear view.

She bit back a hopeful smile and went on with her story.

Oliver took a very roundabout route to make his way to the geriatric ward at seven that evening. It hadn't been possible to locate a plain brown paper bag, so the bag of hamburgers and fries he carried was emblazoned with the red and yellow logo of the world-famous fast-food chain.

A bag he almost dropped when he entered his mother's room. He had expected to find her in her bed. Not sitting in the armchair by the window—wearing her day clothes.

It was nothing short of a miracle.

'You got dressed!'

'Yes…and I feel so much more like myself.' Lady Dorothy smiled at him.

'How on earth…?' The query trailed into silence. He'd been going to ask how she'd managed by herself but that would only be rubbing in the fact that she couldn't. But she hadn't been allowing anybody to help so how...?

'I had some help.' His mother nodded. 'I met the most astonishing girl this afternoon. Bella. Simply delightful.' She gave her son a thoughtful gaze. 'Very pretty, too.'

'Mother!' Oliver shook his head but he was smiling. How could he not smile? This was a major step forward. 'You know my rule about dating nurses. Or doctors. Or anyone else from work. It's a no-go area. Always has been, always will be.'

It wasn't as if he didn't meet countless eligible women through the lavish fundraising occasions he was obliged to attend with his mother and it was rare to find any single woman who wasn't eager to date the Dawson heir. Sex had never been a problem. Finding a woman suitable to produce the grandchild his mother yearned for was quite a different matter, however. It was a search that, quite frankly, Oliver was getting seriously bored by. Or maybe he was resisting because it wasn't just that his mother was yearning for the next generation but that everybody *expected* it to happen.

'Hmmph.' Lady Dorothy sighed. 'Anyway, this Bella used to look after her grandmother who had terrible arthritis so she knows all about it. *She* helped me and... and she managed to do it without making me feel like some kind of oversized infant.'

Oliver made a mental note to find the nurse called Bella and show his appreciation.

'Oh...' His mother bit her lip. 'I meant her nanna, not her grandmother. *She* got murdered.'

'Good grief.' Oliver was setting out the food he'd brought on the end of the bed.

'By her grandfather.'

Oliver's mouth twisted into a wry smile. 'Comes from a good family, then?'

'Don't be a snob, Oliver. She can't help her family any more than any of us can. And she made me laugh.'

'That's wonderful,' Oliver said, and meant it. He screwed up the big paper bag and went to put it in the rubbish bin. There was something large and bright pink filling the metal bucket. He peered closer and then lifted the item out to see what it was.

His mother giggled.

Bella sneaked through the hospital corridors very carefully on her way to the geriatric ward at seven-thirty p.m., a box in her arms.

'Shh...' she said occasionally. 'If we get caught, we're going to be in *big* trouble, Bib.'

Amazingly, she made it to the ward without meeting anybody. The planned treat of letting Lady Dorothy play with a kitten for a few minutes could go ahead. It didn't matter how frozen and sore her hands were right now. She would still be able to feel the softness of this fluffy kitten's fur and have the pleasure of hearing the tiny animal purr.

She tapped softly at the closed door and then let herself in without waiting for a response.

'*Surprise*,' she whispered gleefully.

Except the surprise was hers. Perched on the end of Lady Dorothy's bed, stuffing a hamburger into his mouth, was Oliver Dawson.

CHAPTER THREE

'BELLA!' Lady Dorothy sounded delighted. 'You've come to visit me? What a lovely surprise.'

'*You're* Bella?' Oliver Dawson sounded distinctly less delighted. In fact, he used the hand that wasn't holding the hamburger to cover his eyes as he rubbed his temples with his thumb and middle finger.

'Have you got a headache, darling?' Lady Dorothy asked.

'No.' The word was a growl.

Bella was still staring, dumbfounded. Oliver Dawson was sitting on a patient's bed eating a cheeseburger. A patient who had called him 'darling', no less.

A ripped-open packet of very unhealthy French fries was lying on the bed beside him, the contents well depleted. What's more, he had loosened his tie, undone the top button of his shirt and rolled the sleeves up. Even his hair looked slightly dishevelled. He looked...

Human.

And gorgeous. Gorgeous enough to make Bella's heart skip a beat. And then another. Uh-oh! She recognised that symptom a little too well. It was closely followed, as usual, by that melting sensation deep in her belly that ended with a delicious tingle. The fact that

it was Mr Oliver Dawson she was feeling attracted to
was disturbing to say the least.

'This is my son, Oliver,' Lady Dorothy said. 'Oliver,
this is Bella. I was telling you about her, remember?'

When he took his hand off his eyes, Oliver nodded
wearily. He also looked straight at Bella and she could
swear his colour had heightened and he had a haunted
look in his eyes. He was quite obviously excruciatingly
embarrassed. Well, of course he was. Caught out looking human and eating junk food!

Ha. Finally, she had the advantage.

Sadly, the feeling of one-upmanship lasted precisely
five seconds at which point a scratching noise could
be clearly heard coming from the box in her arms.
Scratching that was followed by a very plaintive miaow.

Lady Dorothy's eyes widened. 'Oh, my goodness…
Did you bring Bib in to visit me?'

'Um…' Bella's gaze slid away from Oliver's but there
was no getting out of this. A tiny paw had appeared in
the centre hole where the flaps of the box didn't quite
meet, as though the kitten was putting her hand up to
be noticed. 'Yes.'

'Show me.' Lady Dorothy tried to shift the bag of
French fries she had on her lap but she couldn't hold
it and it fell, spilling fries onto the floor. Before either
her fumbled movement or the mess could even be com-
mented on, Bella lifted the fluffy grey and white kitten
from the box and deposited her on Lady Dorothy's lap.

Bib, bless her, took one look at the old lady and stood
up on her hind legs, stretching so that she could rub her
head on Lady Dorothy's jawbone. They could all hear

the purring that filled the sudden silence in the room like a miniature chainsaw.

'Oh…*oh*…' Lady Dorothy's voice had a noticeable wobble. 'What a wee darling.' She reached up and it didn't seem to matter that she had to use the back of her hand to stroke the kitten. Bib nimbly climbed a little further, settled into a sphinx-like shape on the platform of a shoulder and started washing the nearest patch of skin she could find. Just beside the diamond stud twinkling in Lady Dorothy's earlobe.

Lady Dorothy sniffed. And smiled, tilting her head to the side a little as a form of caress for the kitten.

Bella had to swallow a lump in her own throat as she observed the pleasure being taken on both sides of the newly formed friendship. When she heard the masculine throat being cleared behind her, she turned in astonishment. Was the poignancy of his mother's joy enough to give him a lump in *his* throat? Maybe he *was* capable of caring about others.

Maybe she was going to have to readjust her opinion of him.

Oliver knew he had to say something but, for the life of him, he couldn't think what.

He'd seen this nurse in pale green, shapeless theatre scrubs with a hat trying to cover her hair. He'd seen her in a dark blue, only slightly less shapeless nurse's uniform, with her hair scraped back and tied into a semblance of submission. When she walked into his mother's room, it was like seeing a totally different woman.

The oversized T-shirt had a neck big enough to

have fallen over one shoulder to reveal a singlet top beneath. Long, long legs were encased in tight leggings and ended with shoes that had impossibly high heels. And the hair was loose. A glorious cascade of golden curls that went halfway down her back and would make any man's fingers itch to bury themselves in its length.

Dear God, what was he thinking? This was the nurse who had elderly patients up line dancing. Who was breaking umpteen rules right now bringing an *animal* into a hospital ward. Who bumped into things and huffed germs all over Theatre because she was clearly distracted by more important things—like the next new pair of shoes, perhaps?

Except that right now she wasn't thinking about shoes. And if she'd brought any germs into the room with that kitten, the risk was more than worth it because his mother had not only forgotten why she was here, she had tears of joy rolling down her cheeks and Oliver had never seen that before. *Ever.*

His mother was not the only one crying either. Bella had turned towards him when he'd cleared his throat a moment ago and those extraordinarily big, blue eyes were shining with moisture. Those full, soft-looking lips were curved into a smile, too. Not the mischievous type of grin they usually looked ready to impart. This was much softer. An expression of empathy and an invitation to share the gift of what was happening with his mother and the kitten.

He really ought to say something. He couldn't sit here staring at her. Not when she was staring back at him and the eye contact had gone on just that shade too long.

An urge to say something about hospital regulations

regarding the lack of visitation rights for pets sprang to mind as Oliver managed to break the eye contact but his gaze fell on the evidence of his appalling dinner still spread over the bed. If his colleagues heard about this, especially the cardiac surgeons, he'd be a laughing stock, and avoiding any such humiliation had always been inbred in any member of the Dawson family.

Oliver sucked in a breath as he looked back at the kitten and then at Bella.

'Ah…could I suggest that whatever happens in Lady Dorothy's room after hours *stays* in Lady Dorothy's room?'

Relief flooded Bella's face, which then lit up with precisely the kind of mischievous grin he knew she'd been capable of. Oddly, it had a glow that he hadn't expected. One that crossed the room and made *him* feel… warm. Happy? Oliver couldn't be sure because it was a very unfamiliar sensation. Definitely not unpleasant, however.

'Sweet,' Bella said. She cast a significant glance at the remnants of fast food and dimples flashed in her cheeks. She was obviously trying not to laugh.

Which was good because it annoyed Oliver and dispersed the strange effect of her smile.

'I'd better go, though,' she added. 'I wouldn't want to get caught by anyone else doing something so illegal.'

'Don't go,' Lady Dorothy begged. 'Not yet.'

'I'll be back tomorrow. I really should take Bib home.'

'But…' There was a vaguely desperate undertone in Lady Dorothy's voice. Oliver found himself holding his breath. Judging by the sudden anxiety on Bella's face, it looked as if she was doing the same thing.

'What is it, Mother?' Oliver prompted gently.

'I...I need some help. To get ready for bed. And...' Her lips were visibly trembling now but her face said it all. It was Bella who she trusted and wanted to help her.

Bella carefully lifted the kitten from where she'd climbed down to go to sleep on Lady Dorothy's lap. 'No worries.' The tone was casual enough to make it seem like no big deal, which seemed to remove any of the embarrassment that was most likely causing his mother's distress. 'I'll put Bib back in her box and then we'll get you sorted.'

Oliver got to his feet. 'I'll get out of the way.' He paused as he got near the door, having kissed his mother's cheek and wished her a good night. He took a final glance at Bella.

What an extraordinary girl she was. Both intensely irritating and utterly remarkable. How did she know exactly what to do or say to make something that couldn't possibly be all right at least acceptable? And how on earth could he thank her for what she'd already done for his mother? Something nobody else had been able to do. Something huge. As big as showing her that life was still worth living?

Something too big to put into words, anyway.

'Thank you, Bella.' The words were totally inadequate. Oliver could only hope that trying to convey his appreciation by holding her eye contact and smiling would be enough.

* * *

That look and that *smile* was still with Bella when she released Bib from the confines of the box, having arrived home at her aunt's house again.

She had done something that Oliver Dawson *approved* of.

How amazing was that?

Not that she'd had any idea that Lady Dorothy was his mother. Just as well she hadn't, really, or she wouldn't have considered doing something as illegal as sneaking a kitten into the ward in a million years.

Right now, she couldn't be more pleased that she'd taken that risk. For once, something had worked out even better than she'd planned and it felt *so* good. Doing something that had pleased Oliver Dawson also felt extraordinarily good. The buzz was making Bella feel unbelievably happy.

Or maybe it was that look from those dark, dark eyes. The look that said she *was* good enough. Special, even. That smile that had gone straight to a point deep in her body and tugged on it.

Oh, help... If she wasn't careful, she'd fall for this surgeon, hook, line and sinker. Bella never had trouble falling in love. She fell out of it again just as easily. But something about that moment of connection felt different.

The waters she could be falling into there were a hell of a lot deeper than any she'd been near before.

Dangerous waters.

She could drown given that the possibility of the potential lifeboat of the attraction being reciprocated to an equal degree was non-existent.

'A bit of fantasy couldn't hurt, though, could it?' she

murmured to Bib as she cuddled the kitten for a moment before putting her down on the floor. 'It's no worse than having the hots for a movie star, is it?'

Bib flicked her pointy little tail and held it straight up like a flag as she trotted down the hallway. Bella looked into the guest suite that was her room. The solitude and opportunity to sit and dream for a while was very attractive but it would be rude not to go and talk to Aunty Kate. She could hear voices in the kitchen. Following them, she found her pathologist aunt barefoot and relaxed, indulging in her favourite pastime of cooking. Her fiancé, orthopaedic surgeon Connor Matthews, was standing behind Kate, his hands resting on her hips and his chin on her shoulder. He was, in fact, nuzzling her aunt's neck.

And Kate was leaning back into the embrace, swaying gently. The pleasure they were both taking from simply being so close to each other was palpable.

Bella suddenly felt like she was intruding into a very private space. One that she couldn't approve of more, given how much real joy Kate's life had been missing before Connor had swept her off her feet and onto the back of his motorbike, but really she should back out and give them the chance to start their lives together without having to worry about an audience.

Connor was the first to notice Bella's arrival.

'Hey! How's it going? Did you find what you'd left at work?'

'Mmm.'

Kate spoke without looking away from the pot she was stirring. 'Really, Bella. You've got to start looking after your stuff a bit more carefully. You'll lose something important one of these days.'

So true. Like her heart, maybe?

Kate gave a squeak then, and looked down. Bib was trying to climb up her jeans. '*Ouch*...where did you spring from? I've been wondering where you'd got to.' She prised the kitten away from her leg and handed her to Connor. 'Could you feed her, please, hon? That way she won't try and eat my leg.' She turned further to smile at Bella. 'You going to eat with us?'

Bella hesitated. 'I don't want to get in the way of you two lovebirds.'

'Don't be daft.' But the look that Kate and Connor exchanged was lingering and very exclusive. Bella couldn't help feeling left out. Lonely, almost.

'How was work?' Kate asked. 'Did you get into any trouble?'

'Almost. I got busted taking a line-dancing class by none other than Oliver Dawson.'

'Uh-oh.' Connor was grinning. 'You really know how to push his buttons, don't you?'

Oh...she wished. If Connor hadn't been there, she might have blurted out the whole story to Kate but the fact that Oliver's mother was an inpatient was being kept under wraps, wasn't it? She'd told Sally she was capable of being discreet. With an enormous effort, Bella put a lid on her inside information.

'What's his deal?' she asked Connor, who had finished scooping cat food into a saucer and had now turned his attention to a rather nice-looking bottle of red wine. 'Why is he so...uptight?'

Connor shrugged. 'Goes with the territory, I guess.'

'What territory?' Bella remembered that Kate had said something similar once about Oliver's background—excusing him when he'd contributed to a bad day by telling her off in public—but she was curious to hear Connor's take on the man. Oddly, she was suddenly aware of a very intense curiosity about anything to do with Oliver Dawson.

'Being a pillar of society. Number one on the rich list. Following in the footsteps of Sir David Matthews can't have been an easy road. Especially when he didn't go into the family business.'

'Which was?'

Connor pulled the cork from the bottle. 'Something that made a serious amount of money. Too many companies to list, probably. Commercial stuff, anyway. I should think it was quite a rebellion to take up medicine.'

'He died a while ago, didn't he?' Kate put in. 'Sir David? I seem to remember that there was some big mystery about it all. Lady Dawson vanished from the social scene anyway and there was a rumour there was more to it than grief.'

'Lady Dorothy.' Bella couldn't help the correction.

Kate raised her eyebrows. 'How do you know her name?'

'Must have heard it mentioned somewhere and remembered,' Bella said vaguely. 'Information is power and all that, you know.'

'Mmm.' Kate was trying not to smile. 'Talking about information…shall we tell her, Connor?'

'Might be a good idea,' he said. 'Seeing as she's going to be chief bridesmaid.'

'The *only* bridesmaid,' Kate shot back. 'This is going to be a quiet affair, remember?'

'Oh, my God...' Bella ran to hug her aunt. 'You've set a date? For the wedding?'

Kate hugged her back, nodding happily. 'In a month's time. I didn't want to risk you deciding to shoot off overseas early or something.'

'Not much chance of that, the way my saving is going.' But Bella shook off the depressing thought. 'This is so cool. Where is it going to be?'

'We're thinking Piha beach.'

'A beach wedding? Excellent. And are you having a honeymoon?'

'For a few days maybe. At a beach where it's a bit safer to swim. Rarotonga or Samoa. Would you be able to cat-sit if we were away?'

'No worries. I'd love to. Ooh...what are you going to wear? Hey...what am *I* going to wear?'

'I'm out of here,' Connor groaned. 'I'll take my wine and go and sit in the garden while you two do the girly thing.' He crossed the kitchen to hand Kate a glass of wine and plant a soft kiss on her lips. 'Call me when dinner's ready?'

Bella watched him go as she took a sip of her own wine. The countdown had really begun. No way could she still be living in this house when these guys came back from their honeymoon.

She'd have to find a flat to share and that meant she'd have to start paying rent. The delicious aroma coming from the pasta sauce Kate was currently creating reminded her that she would have to spend more on food than she was allowed to contribute here as well. If the money in her savings account was going up so slowly now, how much worse would it be when she had to factor in additional living costs? The dreams of going overseas to get her wanderlust out of her system before she settled down to get married and have babies was starting to look like a rather big ask.

Maybe she could get some extra shifts at work. Bella made a mental note to ask Sally about it tomorrow.

'I'm sorry, Bella, as much as I'd like to cure my staffing problems this way, there are rules about how many hours you can do on the trot. Double shifts aren't allowed.'

'OK. It was worth a try.'

Sally sighed. 'I can't even use you on the ward this morning, so I'll have to get a temp in.'

'What?' Bella bit her lip. 'Have I done something wrong? Was it my line-dancing class?' Or had Oliver dobbed her in about sneaking the kitten into the ward last night?

No. As much as she knew he might have liked to do the right thing about breaking such rules, Bella had complete confidence that a promise had been made that would be kept. What had gone on in that room would stay in that room. Maybe that went with all the privileged background stuff too. Bella was quite sure that Oliver Dawson was a man of his word.

Sally laughed. 'Not at all. No...Lady Dorothy apparently pulled some strings and declared that she doesn't want another nurse in her room. You're it.'

'Can she do that?'

'When you come from a family that's supported hospital fundraising to the extent the Dawsons have, I think you can pretty much call the shots. Do you mind?'

'Not at all. I really like her. She reminds me of my nanna.'

'That's good. I get the impression that Lady Dorothy can be formidable if she doesn't get what she's set her heart on.'

What Lady Dorothy had really set her heart on became apparent a little later that morning, after Bella had helped her get dressed and sat with her while the physiotherapist put her through a range of exercises intended to keep her joints mobile. Bella went to fetch Lady Dorothy a cup of the Earl Grey tea she preferred when the session was finished and when she came back, she found that Oliver was visiting his mother.

They seemed to be finishing a rather intense conversation, in fact.

'I can't stop you,' Oliver was saying in a low voice. 'It's your life and your house, after all, but I think it's ill-advised.' When he saw Bella enter the room, he turned away, walking two strides to the outside window where he stood staring at a view she knew was not that fascinating.

Bella had made the tea cool enough to be safe and it was in a cup with a straw.

'Put it there, dear.' Lady Dorothy waved at her bedside table. 'There's something I want to talk to you about.'

Bella set the cup of tea down and turned. She looked at Lady Dorothy sitting up quite straight in her chair. She was smiling. She looked at Oliver's back. He was standing very straight. Bella had the distinct impression that if he turned around, he would not be smiling.

'I want to go home,' Lady Dorothy announced. 'But I realise I'm going to need some help until I get better. Oliver suggested that I get a private nurse.'

'That sounds like a very good idea,' Bella said cautiously, not sure what this had to do with her.

Lady Dorothy beamed at her. 'So you'll take the job, then?'

Bella's jaw dropped. 'I'm not a private nurse. I work here, at St Patrick's.'

'That's what I told you, Mother,' Oliver said, without turning around. 'Private nurses probably have specialised training.'

'Nonsense,' Lady Dorothy said. 'A nurse is a nurse.' She was still smiling at Bella. 'What's to stop you taking on a private job?'

'Oh…no, I couldn't.' Bella was taken aback. 'I'm only working until I can save enough money to go overseas.'

'There you go,' Oliver said. 'You need someone who can commit to more long-term employment.'

'I'd pay you very well, dear.' Lady Oliver frowned at Oliver's back. 'And Oliver won't be in the way. His wing of the house is quite separate, really.'

Bella couldn't help sucking in an audible breath. His *wing* of the house? Her astonishment came out as a rather different query, however. 'You live with your mother?'

The back stiffened further, quite visibly, and Oliver turned to face Bella directly. Oh…Lord…how could she have forgotten just how intimidating this man could be? Except…something about his face reminded her of how he'd looked when she'd caught him out with the fast food. Was he embarrassed by the fact that he still lived with his mother?

Even though the tiny hint of vulnerability was quite appealing, Bella knew it would be a big mistake to smile.

'How long is it going to take for you to save up to go overseas?' Lady Dorothy seemed undeterred.

'Um…a wee while, I guess.' Bella had to look away from the direct stare she was receiving from Oliver. He didn't approve of what his mother was trying to do here. What was the problem? Did he think she wasn't good enough to care for his mother without the kind of supervisory hierarchy a hospital provided? Of course she was. If she wanted to be a private nurse, she would be an excellent one. It was, in fact, the type of job she was considering doing when she went overseas because she'd heard that it paid very well.

'Is that why you live with your aunt? To help you save money?'

'Partly.' Bella turned her attention back to Lady Dorothy who was, after all, a much more likeable person than her son. 'She's also my favourite person in the world. She's not that much older than me and she lived with my family for a long time.' Bella was happy to change the subject because the idea of a job that would pay well enough to speed up her saving was rather tempting.

She also had to admit that Oliver was right. They needed someone who could commit long term. It wouldn't be fair to Lady Dorothy to take on a job as her private nurse and then disappear off overseas in a few months. 'She's getting married soon and I'm going to be her bridesmaid.'

'How exciting. I love weddings. Have you decided what to give them for a gift?'

'No...' Bella hadn't thought about that at all. She wasn't given time to think about it now either because Oliver made a kind of huffing noise and muttered something about having to get back to his ward round.

'I'll see you later, Mother. When I get a chance I'll ring an agency and make some enquiries about private nursing arrangements.'

He nodded at Bella as he left. The matter was ended.

Lady Dorothy left the subject alone for the moment as well, moving on to an animated discussion about potential wedding gifts. Bella's head was whirling with suggestions by the time she headed for her lunch break. Of course she wanted to give Kate and Connor something special but that was going to be awfully expensive, wasn't it?

Bella took a few minutes to surf the internet while she had a coffee to end her break. It seemed like a good idea to try to reconnect with her dreams of overseas travel. She looked at the cost of flights and what she might have to pay for even cheap accommodation in a place like London. She reminded herself that she would need to factor in the cost of eating at least occasionally and allow for it taking a bit of time to find a new job. Then she scribbled on a piece of paper, trying to decide how long it would take her to save enough to spread her wings.

The results were depressing. It might take her a lot

longer than the six months she'd been counting on given her determination to get out of Kate and Connor's way by the time they came back from their honeymoon.

She screwed up the piece of paper and threw it into the bin in the nurses' station. When she went back to Lady Dorothy's room, it seemed like salt was being rubbed into the wound to find her patient brandishing a very similar-looking piece of paper.

'There…' Lady Dorothy was having difficulty keeping hold of the paper but managed to push it towards Bella. 'That's how much I'll pay you to come and be my nurse. I don't care if it's not for very long. I'm sure I'll be much better by the time you want to leave and if I can't manage by myself, I'll come up with another plan.'

Bella took the piece of paper, mainly to save Lady Dorothy the embarrassment of having it fall from her stiff fingers. She caught sight of the amount written in wobbly figures on the paper, however, and her jaw dropped.

'That's ridiculous,' she squeaked. 'You could probably hire three nurses for that much.'

'I don't want three nurses,' Lady Dorothy said firmly. 'I only want one. *You.*'

CHAPTER FOUR

'MOTHER...Bella said she couldn't take the position. Stop pestering her.'

'I'm just trying to understand, Oliver. That can hardly be considered pestering, can it?' The question became directed at Bella as Lady Dorothy turned her head. Her smile was sweet. There was even a dimple flashing in a soft cheek.

Heavens, but she'd changed in the few days Bella had been nursing the elderly lady.

She couldn't help smiling back but she said nothing, merely continuing the task of folding and packing Lady Dorothy's clothes in preparation for her discharge.

Oliver Dawson picked up a book and moved to put it in the suitcase beside Bella.

'Sweet as they come on the outside,' he murmured, 'but you have probably noticed that my mother has a core of reinforced steel.'

Bella caught her bottom lip between her teeth to stop herself laughing aloud as her gaze flew up to meet his. This was a surprise visit and he obviously hadn't finished his theatre list because he was still wearing scrubs. He even had a red mark on his forehead from recent, and probably lengthy, contact with the elastic edge of a theatre cap. Having Oliver dressed like this was quite enough to put Bella back into a space of feeling very nervous. She would make some idiotic mistake any moment now and have to bear the consequences. A mistake like thinking he was making a *joke* about his mother?

There was no mistaking the glimmer of humour in those dark eyes, however, and Bella felt suddenly confused. Thrown off balance. It was as much of a surprise as finding the eminent surgeon sitting on a bed and eating disreputable fast food.

'I'll bet the campaign has been going on for the last three days, am I right?'

Bella made a choked sound that could have been agreement. She was finding it disturbingly hard to look away from that totally unexpected humour.

'Just tell me again, dear,' Lady Dorothy's voice came from behind them. Her voice had the faintest hint of a plaintive wobble. 'Time's running out now.'

Bella turned back to the bed. 'It wouldn't be fair to sign on as your private nurse. I'm not going to be in Auckland for much longer.'

'But where are you going?'

'Overseas,' Bella said firmly. 'I told you all about it yesterday.'

'Mmm.' Lady Dorothy was smiling again. 'But you made it sound like it was just a holiday, not something… urgent.'

Bella tried to see beneath the sweet smile and the sincere interest that had had her talking about herself for days now. Had Oliver been warning her that his mother was still embarked on a campaign to get what she had decided she wanted?

'It's my time to travel,' Bella said. She tried to keep an apologetic note from her voice but this was making her feel guilty. She had become enormously fond of Lady Dorothy over the last few days. She'd love to give her exactly what she wanted but it simply wasn't possible. 'And it *is* urgent because if I don't go now, I never will.'

'Of course you will, dear. Europe isn't going to disappear, you know.'

She really didn't understand. Bella sank onto the chair beside the bed, only too aware of Oliver standing at the end of the bed.

'I had planned to go when I left home,' Bella told Lady Dorothy. 'But that was when Nanna came to live with us and I couldn't leave. And then I did my nursing degree and ever since then I've been trying to save up enough to go but...' She didn't need to go into details in front of Oliver about how bad she was at saving her money, did she? Confess to the impulsiveness that made a new dress or killer pair of shoes an absolute must-have? 'Anyway, that's why I came to Auckland. So I could live with Auntie Kate and finally save enough to get away.'

She could see that this argument wasn't hitting the right note. She could almost see Lady Dorothy gathering her breath to tell her again that if she became her private nurse, she could save the money she needed in no time. She'd dropped that subject the other night and had distracted Bella into talking about weddings but it hadn't gone away, had it? Maybe she'd been simply gathering more ammunition so that she could fire it all at the same time.

'And it's urgent now,' Bella continued, 'because I'm twenty-six. Going on twenty-seven, in fact, and I intend to be married and having my first baby by the time I'm thirty. And I want to spend at least three or four years travelling the world,' she added with a touch of desperation.

'Oh, my…' Lady Dorothy's eyes were wide. 'You have a fiancé?'

'No.' Bella closed her eyes for a moment, wishing Oliver would go away. 'Not yet,' she muttered.

She opened her eyes to see that Lady Dorothy was looking at her son and that she was smiling again.

Oliver also muttered something that sounded remarkably like *give me strength*.

Good grief…surely Lady Dorothy didn't think that Oliver would be remotely interested in the fact that she was single? How embarrassing!

'Quite apart from that,' Bella said crisply, 'I'm not qualified. I don't know about the kind of rehabilitation programme you're going to need. Occupational therapy and so on.'

'We can learn together, then,' Lady Dorothy said calmly. 'You already know far more than I do, dear. Because of your nanna.'

'There's physiotherapy, then. Specialist exercises.'

'We could learn those together, too. And—' Lady Dorothy's eyes twinkled '—maybe I want to learn line dancing.'

Oliver did more than mutter this time. He actually groaned.

Bella ignored that one. 'Physios have access to things that you might need. Like hot pools.'

'We have a hot pool at home, don't we, Oliver? There's a spa beside the indoor swimming pool.'

There was an indoor swimming pool? Separate wings of the house? There were probably converted servants' quarters that would be available as a private apartment, too. Bella's head was spinning slightly.

It stopped spinning abruptly, thanks to the loud crash directly outside Lady Dorothy's door.

There was a moment's shocked silence inside the room and then Oliver took two long strides and flung the door open.

'What the—?'

Bella didn't let him finish his outraged query about what might be going on because she'd seen the figure on the floor.

'Oh, my God… *Wally.*'

Her favourite line-dancing pupil had collapsed and he was lying flat on his back. Bella flew to his side.

'Wally? Can you hear me?'

There was no response. Automatically, Bella reached for the elderly man's head, tipping it back to ensure his airway was open. She bent down to listen for breathing, one hand on his neck to search for a pulse. She was ready to start CPR instantly if she couldn't find one. Her adrenaline level was sky-high. Why on earth was Oliver just standing there? He wasn't even calling for extra assistance yet.

'Let him go, Bella.' Oliver spoke calmly. 'Stand back.'

Her jaw dropped. He wanted her to stand back and

let her patient die? Why? Because he was old or overweight or deaf or something?

'No way.' Bella glared at Oliver. 'He needs *help*.' Even as she spoke, however, Bella could feel something happening beneath her hands. An ominous twitching and jerking. Wally was having a seizure.

Bella knew better than to try and restrain someone who was having a seizure. There was nothing anyone could do until it stopped, other than try and protect the head from banging into something. When the uncontrolled movements stopped she would be able to ensure that his airway stayed clear and that he wouldn't be frightened in that confused period before full consciousness returned.

'Move that trolley,' she heard herself order Oliver. 'I'll find a towel to go under his head.'

She grabbed one from the rail in Lady Dorothy's room and was back within seconds.

Wally was still having his seizure. The longer it went on the more serious it was likely to be and it looked quite bad enough already. Wally must have bitten his tongue because there was blood-stained foam coming from his mouth. What if he was in *status epilepticus*? Oliver was signalling another nurse and calling for a drug trolley.

'I should have done something this morning,' Bella groaned. 'I told Sally I thought he needed a scan or something.'

'What?' Oliver was close beside where Bella was crouching now. 'What are you talking about?'

'He's been having headaches and this morning he said his vision was blurry. And now this...' Bella could feel tears stinging the back of her eyes as she looked up at Oliver. 'He might have a brain tumour, mightn't he?'

'So you're a neurosurgeon now?' But the words were not sarcastic. If anything, the look that Oliver gave her was reassuring. And there was something else in his glance. Something that made Bella feel oddly warm. Had he been impressed with the way she had handled this emergency?

'We'll have a good look at him, Bella, and find out what's going on. I take it he doesn't have a history of seizures?'

Bella shook her head. A nurse had arrived with the drug trolley but it seemed that chemical intervention wasn't going to be necessary to halt the seizing. Wally was lying still now. Bella wriggled to where she could control his airway and cushion his head with the towel. She used a corner of it to wipe the foam from his chin.

Wally groaned.

'It's OK,' Bella told him. 'You're safe, Wally.' She stroked his forehead. 'We're looking after you. It's OK.'

'Find a stretcher,' Oliver ordered another staff member. 'And call CT and see if they can fit in an emergency case.'

Bella almost gasped. Oliver was going to look at Wally right now? Her smile wobbled a little.

'Thank you so much,' she whispered. 'I know he's getting on but he's such a sweetheart and I know he's deaf but he's still as sharp as a tack.'

Oliver had hold of Wally's wrist, taking his pulse. 'You're really fond of him, aren't you?'

Bella nodded. 'I didn't expect to enjoy Geriatrics this much,' she confessed, 'but you know what?'

'What?'

'They're as good as babies in their own way. You can't help loving them.'

Wally was coming out of his post-ictal state reasonably quickly. With plenty of assistance, staff got him onto a stretcher and ready to be taken to the CT lab.

'Go with him.' Lady Dorothy had been watching the drama from her bed and anyone could see that Bella was torn when she went back into her patient's room. 'I'm fine.'

'Go,' Oliver agreed. 'I'll come down and see what the results are as soon as I can.' He lifted a hand in farewell to his mother and followed Bella out of the door.

'About before,' he said quietly. 'You have every right to say no to my mother. And if you have any doubts about accepting the position she's offering, that's exactly what you *should* say.'

If *she* had any doubts?

What about *his* doubts? The frank disapproval that had radiated from him the other night when Lady Dorothy had first mooted the subject? Had he changed his mind? He couldn't have missed the bond that had developed between herself and his mother over the last few days and Oliver Dawson clearly loved his mother. And he'd witnessed her dealing with an emergency with another patient today. Did he, in fact, think she might be the right person for this important job now?

Approve of her, even?

The very idea made her head spin all over again. Why was it suddenly such a desirable thing to have Oliver approve of her? Bella tried to shake it off as being no more than a way of redeeming herself for the klutzy mistakes she seemed to have been programmed to make in front of him up till now. A desire to prove that she wasn't incompetent and irresponsible. The way she had today?

Wally had had his scan now. A procedure that had shown Bella's inexpert diagnosis to be correct. There was a growth in the elderly man's head that was causing his symptoms. He was scheduled for an MRI scan and the more detailed results would determine whether the tumour was operable.

He was resting comfortably in his own room now and Bella was back with Lady Dorothy, testing her blood-sugar levels again.

She couldn't stop thinking about what Oliver had said, though. And now she was fighting a desire to win more of his approval.

It pulled her back in time. To those way too familiar episodes of being desperate to win back the approval of her father. Or Kate. But, then, Oliver wasn't family. She wasn't even attracted to him, except in that pining after a movie-star, *unattainable* kind of way.

Letting herself think for a moment that that unattainability might be up for negotiation was guaranteed to make her head spin to a degree where she might do something really silly so Bella made a determined effort to plant herself firmly back in reality. She focussed on what Lady Dorothy was now saying. Oliver had been right. His mother wasn't giving up on trying to persuade her to become her private nurse.

'You'd love it, I promise. We have access to a beach that's so cut off other people can only get to it by boat so it's virtually private. And…' Lady Dorothy reached out to touch Bella's hand '…it would mean so much, dear. To both me and Oliver.'

Really?

'Your son thinks I'm an idiot,' Bella heard herself blurt out. Well, maybe he didn't think she was quite as stupid as he had done but it wouldn't take much to wipe out the better impression he'd gained today, would it? Bella knew perfectly well she was highly likely to do something else that he would think ill-considered. Or irresponsible.

Lady Dorothy was silent for a moment. 'Oliver didn't have the happiest childhood,' she said then. 'He learned self-control and responsibility at an age when most children were simply having fun.'

She sounded sad about it. As though she considered it a failing on her part as a mother. Bella found herself curling her own hand around Lady Dorothy's. Very gently, so she didn't hurt the still red, swollen joints.

Oliver had had an unhappy childhood? Bella had always found that sadness was very contagious.

'He's brilliant at what he does,' Lady Dorothy continued, 'and I couldn't be more proud of him but…' She lowered her voice. 'He's just a little bit *stuffy*, don't you think?'

Bella gasped. This was as outrageous as Oliver making jokes about his mother.

In fact, there was an amused gleam in Lady Dorothy's eyes that reminded her very strongly of the one she'd seen in Oliver's.

'It would do him good to get shaken up a little,' Lady Dorothy murmured. 'To have some fun.'

Oh…but that concept appealed to Bella no end. The streak of mischief that she knew she really ought to grow out of was firing up right now. Alert and sending delicious, persuasive bursts of energy through her body. Teasing Oliver Dawson?

It had often worked with her father.

And Kate.

But to try it on Oliver? No-o-o. It would be like playing with fire. Lighting matches near something when she had no idea what the result might be.

A disappointing fizzle?

A conflagration?

An explosion that could cause all manner of collateral damage?

Hmm. Not a good idea. That temptation would have to be filed under the other reasons that weren't quite morally acceptable.

Like solving the problem of moving out of Kate's house to give her and Connor some privacy as they started the rest of their lives together.

Like living in some amazing mansion that had an indoor swimming pool and a private beach.

Like having enough money to make her overseas experience one long holiday instead of small snatches of time sandwiched between jobs.

Bella was still holding Lady Dorothy's hand. Stroking it very, very gently. Feeling the shape of her joints and knowing how much pain and frustration they were causing her.

And then she looked up and caught Lady Dorothy's gaze and suddenly everything fell into place with a very obvious clunk.

This wasn't about any financial incentives.

It wasn't about Oliver Dawson.

It was about a woman who just happened to be his mother and the look in this elderly woman's eyes. The plea in them. It could be her beloved nanna looking at her right now.

She'd been too late to do much for Nanna. To help her get to a space where she could still have a good quality of life for however many years she had left. But she could do it for Lady Dorothy.

She wanted to do it. More than she wanted anything else that was on the immediate agenda, like working with babies or heading for Europe. Six months would be long enough to make a real difference, wouldn't it?

It seemed long enough to be able to accomplish anything.

'I'll do it,' she said softly. 'I'd really like to be your nurse, Lady Dorothy.'

CHAPTER FIVE

IT HAD been one of those days.

Oliver Dawson wanted nothing more than to retreat to his favourite place in the world—the old, slightly ramshackle summer house that had been tucked into the cliffside at the bottom of the garden, just beside the steep, overgrown steps that led down to the beach.

The semicircle skeleton of iron and wood had long since been taken over by roses and jasmine and honeysuckle and at almost any time of the year there was a glorious perfume. The built-in seating was wide enough to be used as a bed and if the cushions were well past their use-by date, it didn't matter a bit. Not when the view was so compelling. Mile after mile of sea. A view that pulled you into its enormity and made everything else irrelevant.

A place of complete relaxation. No pressure. No disappointments. No expectations at all, just a blessed nothingness. Exactly what he needed after a day like today.

Not that he was complaining, of course. Having a crisis appear from nowhere and demand so much skill and concentration that he was left feeling drained was precisely the kind of thing that had drawn him to neurosurgery in the first place.

It had been fifteen-year-old Tyler this afternoon. The innocent victim of a gang-related drive-by shooting, he'd had surgery for his head injury two days ago. Routine surgery. All it had needed had been a bit of debridement and a careful check to make sure there was no major damage. And there hadn't been. Tyler had been incredibly lucky.

When he'd had a seizure completely out of the blue that afternoon, Oliver had been paged instantly. He'd arrived to find the boy's level of consciousness had deteriorated and there were other ominous signs, like the one-sided drift when he was asked to close his eyes and hold his hands palms upwards. The diagnosis had been obvious. A post-op bleed happening just behind the surgery site had been an emergency that couldn't wait a minute longer than absolutely necessary. A theatre had needed to be found and staffed. They'd had to lift the bone flap, excavate the clot, find the source of the bleeding and make sure it stopped.

It had been a battle with a time limit and the tension had made the case all the more exhausting to end a day with.

All the more satisfying that it had appeared to have been successful but Oliver wouldn't be completely satisfied until he was sure that Tyler hadn't been left with any lingering neurology and it was still too soon to tell. That meant that some of the tension was still with him. The buzz of the race against time was still there too. He might be absolutely drained but Oliver was still far too wired to relax. He needed the summer house. Maybe a good workout in the gym first, to get rid of the kink in his neck and the ache in his back and to burn off the last of the adrenaline he could still feel coursing through his body. He knew exactly what he needed to do in order to centre himself again because it was a well-practised and cherished routine.

Having parked his luxurious but entirely practical BMW sedan in the garage complex, Oliver opened the front door of his house, threw the keys into the antique beaten silver bowl on the hall stand and then stopped dead in his tracks.

He could hear music.

Country music.

He actually closed his eyes for a long, long moment. In the comfort to be found in anticipating his wind-down routine, he had completely forgotten how much things had changed in his home.

His mother was still in the early stages of rehabilitation and coming to terms with any new limitations she would be left with. He couldn't just greet her in passing, knowing that she understood that he would be back to spend time with her when he'd dealt with any aftermath of his demanding job.

And that was only the thin edge of the wedge of change. Bella was living there. She had been there for a week now. And she was the only person who could possibly be responsible for the sound of Johnny Cash wafting from the conservatory. Part of Oliver wanted nothing more than to block his ears and ignore the sound but he knew it was impossible. Just as impossible as ignoring the fact that Bella Graham was living in his house.

If he'd had the slightest inkling of how pervasive her presence would be, he would have somehow talked his mother into hiring another nurse. He only had himself to blame, didn't he? He'd been entranced by the instinctive people skills Bella seemed to possess and then he'd been overwhelmed by a sense of relief that a way forward, albeit temporary, had been found. One that was making his mother happier than he had seen her for a long, long time, which was extraordinary, given what she was having to deal with now.

He'd thought it wouldn't impinge on his own life at all. His own wing was virtually self-contained and he could eat out instead of using the main kitchen facilities. Surely Bella wouldn't be on duty twenty-four seven so he probably wouldn't encounter her very often when he popped in every day to check on his mother.

How naive had he been?

Bella's presence was like…a sound or a scent or something. It trickled into and lingered in spaces she hadn't even entered. It bubbled and fizzed in odd corners with an effervescence that was disturbingly refreshing. It made his mother happy so he was quite prepared to tolerate it.

But Johnny Cash?

Not acceptable. On any level.

Lady Dorothy had finally nailed The Electric Slide.

Bella was grinning from ear to ear as she held up her hand. 'High-five,' she commanded. 'You are a *legend*.'

How many seventy-something women would be prepared to high-five someone? Bella's grin widened even further as her palm made contact—gently—with Lady Dorothy's.

How many would be determined to learn to line

dance, for that matter? Or be prepared to throw herself into rehabilitation with the kind of guts that her private patient was demonstrating? This was already the most rewarding job she'd ever had and if Lady Dorothy kept up the kind of progress she'd made in the last week, Bella's plans to head overseas in six months' time wouldn't need to be disrupted at all.

'Let's do it once more,' Lady Dorothy said. 'So I don't forget by tomorrow.'

'No worries. Some more Johnny Cash?'

'No. Let's have that "Achy-breaky heart" again.'

The smooth tones of Billy Ray Cyrus filled the conservatory and Bella took her place beside Lady Dorothy.

'OK. Step right. Cross behind with the left foot. Right foot out. Stomp left and *clap*.' Bella made her clap extra loud to make up for the fact that Lady Dorothy wasn't allowed to risk injuring the healing joints in her fingers. She even added a 'Woohoo!' as they turned to face the next wall and do the short routine again.

Only they both stopped before the next step right.

Staring at them from the door of the conservatory was Oliver.

'Hello, darling.' Lady Dorothy raised her voice to be heard over Billy Ray. 'You're just in time. Come and join us.'

Bella could see the balloon over Oliver's head that had *Not in this lifetime* printed inside it.

'Please,' Lady Dorothy said. 'It's not really *line* dancing when there's only two of us.'

The request was sweet but Bella could detect the determination not to accept no for an answer. What had Oliver said about his mother having a core of re-inforced steel?

Come to that, what had Lady Dorothy said about her son needing to be shaken up a little? To be forced to have some fun?

And what better fun was there than line dancing?

'Come on.' Bella tried her most winning smile. 'You're a brain surgeon. This will be a doddle.'

'It'll only take a couple of minutes.' Lady Dorothy was sounding firmer now. 'I want to show you how good my balance is getting.'

'I'll watch from here.'

'Oh, don't be so stuffy, Oliver,' Lady Dorothy said. 'It's *fun*.'

Bella hid her smile as she saw Oliver's chest heave in a long-suffering sigh before he discarded his jacket, loosened his tie and rolled his sleeves up.

'Five minutes,' he growled. 'I've got a workout to get to.'

This was obviously something that was so far out of Oliver Dawson's comfort zone Bella almost felt sorry for him.

But it would do him good, she decided. He might be a brilliant surgeon and he definitely loved his mother and that was all very commendable but there was no denying that he *was* stuffy.

He needed shaking up and she was just the woman to do it.

Bella beamed at Oliver. 'Follow our steps. We just turn three hundred and sixty degrees and do this little routine at each turn. Ready? OK. Step right, like this...'

* * *

This was torture.

Demeaning and ridiculous. He should have just put his foot down and excused himself instead of being sucked in by the plea in his mother's face. Hadn't he grown up to enough to realise that pleasing himself was more important than pleasing a parent?

Apparently not.

It wasn't the best mind set to be in for following the directions of a girl who seemed to have life organised to deliver precisely what would please herself more than anyone else.

She was just so damn...*joyful*.

She wasn't required to wear a uniform in this new position of hers and right now she was wearing some rather tight-fitting jeans and a white top that looked like it belonged to a gypsy. All ruffles and elastic, including a tight line under her breasts and a ruffle around the neckline that did nothing to hide her cleavage. She didn't have to confine her hair either, but at least it was half-up and not that uncontrolled cascade of curls that had made his fingers itch the first time he'd seen it.

Or maybe it wasn't any better. As Oliver gritted his teeth and followed the stupid stepping and clapping instructions, Bella suddenly whirled a quarter turn and her hair swirled with her. At least half of it was scraped back loosely from her face and pinned high on the back of her head with a sparkly clip. All Oliver could think now was how much better it would look if someone pulled that clip out and let the whole lot ripple over her shoulders and down her back. The back of that top was just as low as the front. He could see an expanse of smooth, golden-brown skin.

'You forgot to clap,' Bella admonished him, with a grin. 'On every count of four, remember?'

Oliver froze in mid-step. He hadn't wanted to do this in the first place. He needed time to himself to unwind and enjoy being in his own home, doing what *he* chose to do.

He really didn't want to be dancing—if this silly stepping really counted as such an activity.

He also really, *really* didn't want to be aware of any physical attraction that his mother's nurse might possess.

And now he was being told he wasn't doing it right? That he wasn't performing up to expectations? Did Bella share his mother's opinion that he was *stuffy*? The way she was smiling right now suggested that something was certainly amusing her.

That did it. With a look that had been known to send junior nurses fleeing his operating theatre in tears, Oliver turned on his heel and left the room.

'Forty-nine….*fifty*…' With an agonised grunt, Oliver let the weights on the bench press drop with a resounding clank.

He was dripping with sweat. He'd put the weights up on every machine and driven himself harder than he ever had but the tension he was feeling hadn't gone away one bit.

Maybe a run would do the trick. The state-of-the-art treadmill in the corner of gym could be adjusted in both speed and incline until it felt like you were trying to run up a cliff side. It was also positioned so that you could look out at the sea while you were running but Oliver wasn't even aware of the glorious view this evening.

He was still angry at having been pushed so far out of his comfort zone.

He'd hated it.

Or maybe he hadn't and that was the real problem here.

Did he really come across to everyone as being stuffy?

Did he care?

Maybe he did. Bella was the opposite of stuffy. She was the kind of person he'd always envied when he'd been at school. The popular type who always seemed to be having fun. Normal rules didn't seem to apply to those golden people. They were the rebels that got away with breaking the rules. The ones who seemed to lead a charmed life.

Oliver's breath was coming in such short, painful gasps he was forced to reduce the incline on the treadmill.

The only rebellion he'd ever attempted had been to go to medical school instead of the position waiting for him in one of his father's *über*-successful businesses. That had nearly been enough to make public the sham of the Dawsons' happy family image so the pressure had been on to prove himself after that. Not only to succeed but to do it so well that nobody could point a finger and say that his father had been right in his opposition.

And that had meant keeping himself apart from the other medical students. The ones that got drunk and partied to relieve the stress. The ones that competed to see who got the prettiest nurses first.

Nurses like Bella.

With a groan, Oliver let the treadmill wind down. He stripped off his sweat-sodden T-shirt, his trainers and his socks but he left his boxer shorts on. A few rapid strides and he could dive into the welcome coolness of the indoor pool. When he surfaced, he immediately began a strong overarm stroke that pulled him quickly to the other end of the pool. Then he ducked and rolled, using his feet to push him off the side to begin the next length.

And still the tension bubbled inside his head.

He *was* stuffy. Good grief...he was only thirty-six years old but he was middle-aged to the nth degree. Had been since God knew when.

Had he entered a middle-aged mentality when he'd been in his teens? When he'd decided that both his father's personality and his behaviour simply wasn't acceptable?

Or had it been even earlier than that? When he'd seen that his mother needed protection?

Needed genuine love.

Oliver swam another length. And another. Maybe he needed to dry himself off and go and sit in the summer house for a while to finally get rid of this unpleasant feeling of...what was it?

Frustration?

A dislike of who he was?

No. It was more a sense of having missed out on something important.

That he was still missing out.

And not knowing quite what it was that he was missing out on.

* * *

The spa pool was set into the gym set-up on the lower floor of the Dawson mansion.

Lady Dorothy had taken some persuasion to don a bathing suit and start some water therapy but the visiting physio had recommended it and Bella had gone home to Kate's house last night to fetch her own bathing suit so that she could do more than supervise from the edge of the pool.

Finally, she had Lady Dorothy seated safely in the pool.

'Don't get a fright,' she warned. 'I'm going to turn the jets on now.'

The pool hummed into life and the pressure of the moving water increased around them.

'Good heavens!' Lady Dorothy exclaimed. 'This is… extraordinary.'

Bella blinked. 'Haven't you been in a spa pool before?'

'Never. This is Oliver's playroom, not mine.'

Bella took another long glance around them. Yep. She was still blown away by what looked like the ultimate home fitness area. The room was vast. It probably took up the lower floor of this whole wing. The pool had to be fifty feet long and the dark blue tiling made the water match what she could see of the ocean through the windows.

No waves, though. The pool lay like a giant mirror, with faint curls of steam rising from its glassy surface. Both the swimming pool and the spa pool were at a level that made them in line with the expanse of the sea. At the far end of the pool was a treadmill that was also positioned for the view.

An infinity treadmill. Who knew?

'Not much of a playroom,' she said aloud. 'It looks like a torture chamber with all those machines. Oliver must be very fit.'

'His father got terribly overweight,' Lady Dorothy responded. 'That's what caused his heart attack, of course. Just one of the attributes Oliver didn't want to emulate, I expect.'

Bella was surprised again. What a cryptic thing to say. She really wanted to ask what else about his father he hadn't liked but, for once, she paid heed to the warning bell.

She'd already gone too far, hadn't she, pushing Oliver with that line dancing the other night? He'd been absolutely furious with her and she had been keeping her head down and avoiding him ever since. When he came to visit his mother in the evenings, she made sure that there was some urgent task she simply had to get done. And last night she'd been out for hours, having dinner with Kate and Connor.

She'd told them about making St Patrick's head neurosurgeon line dance and Kate had shaken her head.

'You'll get yourself into trouble, Bella. You might lose this job if you're not careful.'

'I won't. Lady Dorothy loves me and she's doing really well. I'm right on top of supervising her diabetes. Oliver said that he's never seen her blood-glucose levels under such tight control.'

'Oh...*Oliver* now, is it?'

'Not to his face,' Bella had to confess. 'I haven't got the nerve but it would seem silly to call him Mr Dawson in his own home, wouldn't it?'

'I'd check first,' Kate advised. 'And possibly not while you're making him do something as embarrassing as line dancing.'

The cringe factor was still there. With a sigh, Bella forced herself to focus.

'Put your arms out so that your fingers are in the bubbles,' she told Lady Dorothy. 'Then we'll see how we go with your exercises.'

'Do you think I should take my necklace off, dear? I'm a bit worried about what the chemicals might do to the stones. I'm sure I can smell chlorine.'

'I don't think it will hurt your necklace.'

'I rather not risk it. Could you do the clasp for me, please, Bella?'

'Sure.' Bella unclipped the string of polished garnets that was one of Lady Dorothy's favourites. So much so that her new employer was planning to measure the success of her progress by when she would be able to wear the matching ring again.

And Bella had every intention of helping her to do just that. That was what she was there for and it would be best if she stopped thinking about Oliver Dawson at all.

Unfortunately, it wasn't that easy. Even knowing that she had infuriated him didn't seem to be enough to quell the temptation to go there again. Maybe it enhanced it, even.

It was a personality flaw, wasn't it? To be scared of something but drawn to the danger of it?

Exactly the kind of situation that had got Bella into trouble all her life. Doing something again when she knew she shouldn't because she just had to find out what would happen if she did.

Honestly, she should have grown out of it by now because she'd had plenty of examples when the thing that had happened had been bad.

Like all the toys she had broken as a child because she'd just had to bend them in an impossible direction or see if they could survive being dropped out of a window or something. In the end, her father had been so angry her pocket money had been stopped until she learned better sense.

And what about when she'd broken her arm falling out of that tree when she'd gone out on a branch that obviously didn't have the strength to support her?

Or the time she'd nearly drowned and the lifeguards had had to rescue her from the hole in the surf with its lethal swirl of competing currents?

That had been at Piha.

Now, there was a distraction. Bella helped Lady Dorothy flex and straighten her fingers in the hot current of moving water. The upcoming wedding that was to happen at Piha beach.

'That's fantastic,' she encouraged Lady Dorothy. 'Look, they're much straighter than they were yesterday. Can you do your wrist exercises too?'

The movements were almost routine now. Lady Dorothy had been right. They were learning together and Bella knew she was already far more qualified than she had been when she had been trying to help look after her nanna.

Which was such a shame because if Nanna were here

now, she would be so excited about Kate's wedding, which was only a few weeks away now.

Bella was excited.

So was Connor.

Even Lady Dorothy kept asking about how the plans for the beach wedding were going.

The only person who didn't seem over the moon about it, Bella had decided last night, was Kate.

Which was odd. Disturbing, even. Connor hadn't seemed to notice anything amiss but, in some ways, he didn't know Kate as well as Bella did, did he?

She'd known her aunt since she'd been a small girl and Kate had been a troubled teen who had come from an appallingly abusive background. Her father had been a violent bastard and her mother had failed to protect Kate other than by sending her away to live with her much older brother's family. And then her father had murdered her mother and been sent to prison for it!

Not that Bella had known that until recently but she had known that Kate had secrets. She'd always known that some things were tucked away and hidden so well that sometimes Bella was the only one who could see that locked door in Kate's eyes. She'd seen the bone-deep sadness that could only be the aftermath of something really bad happening.

And she thought she'd seen it again last night for the first time in many years.

Maybe she was wrong. Bella hoped she was wrong but it needed thinking about, didn't it?

And worrying about her aunt was the probably the only sure-fire way she could distract herself completely from thinking about Oliver.

If shades of the past were haunting Kate again it couldn't have anything to do with her father because he was gone. Locked away so securely he would never see freedom again for as long as he lived.

Had Connor done something to remind Kate of her father?

No. Simply not possible. OK, Connor was big and powerful and wore leathers and rode a motorbike but if there was any propensity for violence it would have come out when he'd seen Kate being attacked by her father in the pathology lab that day.

A curl of shame always came with that memory for Bella. It had been her fault the situation had happened in the first place. She'd irresponsibly jumped in and arranged the meeting, thinking she could resolve old family issues, and it had led to disaster.

Well…not complete disaster. After all, it had been precisely that situation that had shown both Kate and Connor how much in love with each other they were and now here they were, planning their wedding and the rest of their lives together.

Lady Dorothy was wriggling her fingers as if she was playing a piano now.

'They hardly hurt at all,' she said happily.

'Excellent. Let's work on your wrists now.'

Bella helped with the movements but her thoughts were drawn back to the problem at hand. She needed to focus.

Pride in her part in bringing her beloved aunt and her lover to the point where they were sublimely happy was beside the point because Kate wasn't so happy any more. And Bella was quite sure it wasn't anything

Connor might have said or done. He hadn't shown any violence towards her grandfather in the lab that day when he'd clearly deserved it. No. He'd used his strength and his big body to shield Kate and protect her. So it couldn't be that something had happened in their relationship to remind Kate of her past.

No way.

So it had to be something else.

But what?

CHAPTER SIX

'EVERYTHING'S fine, Bella.'

'Are you sure?'

'Of course I'm sure. Where's this coming from?'

There was a short silence on the other end of the line. 'Um…' It wasn't like Bella to sound so unsure of herself. 'It's just a feeling I got the other night and it won't go away. Like you're hiding something.'

Kate froze. If Bella suspected something, how long would it be before Connor did? She stopped sorting the papers on the desk in front of her and raised her head to stare through the glass windows of her office into St Patrick's busy pathology lab. No. She was sure Connor didn't suspect anything. His lovemaking last night had been the usual mix of raw masculine power and the gentleness that could bring her to tears if she thought about it.

Like now. Kate had to blink hard.

'Kate?'

'I'm here.' Kate cleared her throat and tried to swallow but her mouth felt strangely dry. The person she loved most in the world after Connor had to be her niece. The bond they had was unique and ran deep. It went back to a time when Kate had had dark secrets to hide and Bella was far too young to know about any of them. She knew more now but she still didn't know everything. And she wasn't going to, any more than Connor was.

Kate was starting a new life. A future that was more than anything she'd ever dreamed of. Marriage to a man she would die for. A man who, miraculously, seemed to love her just as much.

The past was gone. Or was it? Maybe that was why Bella was asking awkward questions. She'd known Kate a lot longer than Connor had so maybe she was tuned in at a different level. Something like panic opened its claws in Kate's belly. She had to stop the direction of this conversation urgently. Before it did her head in and she said something that would blow the whole can of worms open.

'I'm pretty busy, hon. Was there something in particular you wanted to talk about?'

She heard a sigh. 'I'm not having a great day, I guess. I've been worried about you and—'

'Well, you can stop worrying about me for a start.' Kate interrupted firmly.

'But...' Clearly, Bella wasn't going to be reassured that easily.

'I don't know what you think you've picked up, but it's probably just a bit of pre-wedding jitters or something.'

'Jitters? How can you have jitters when you're getting married to Connor? He's gorgeous. And he adores you. You adore him. You're perfect for each other. If I'm half as lucky as you, then I'll be happy.'

'It's getting close rapidly, that's all.' Maybe there

was a way forward to be found here. A means of buying time? Softening the final blow that had to come?

'I'm just wondering if we're rushing things a bit.'

There was a horrified silence coming down the phone. Kate had to think quickly and change the subject. Before something catastrophic happened, like her bursting into tears. Desperately, she grabbed a conversational lifeline.

'Why else are you having a bad day? Apart from anything to do with me?'

'What? Oh…I can't find Lady Dorothy's necklace.'

Relief flooded Kate. Here was her reprieve. 'Oh, my God…have you lost a string of priceless Dawson diamonds or something?'

'Not diamonds. Garnets. And I haven't *lost* it. I've just…misplaced it. Only it's Lady Dorothy's favourite and she's kind of upset.'

'Where did you last see it?' Kate was idly sorting papers again, confident that she'd headed Bella off from dangerous territory. Good grief, but these path results that needed her attention were piling up. Some had been sitting on her desk for weeks and weeks now. Well, that one could go. She screwed up a copy of a result that she had made a note on about getting the calibration of a machine checked. The task had long since been done.

'I took it off for her when we were in the spa pool the other day but I know I picked it up afterwards. We just didn't stop to put it back on because she was a bit cold and I wanted to get her dressed again.'

'So you must have dropped it somewhere. Retrace your steps.'

Always the best idea. Go back to the point you started

from and find out where things had gone wrong. Bella seemed to be explaining that she'd done exactly that but her voice was no more than a background buzz in Kate's ear now.

She had unearthed a scrap of paper at the very bottom of that pile from the corner of her desk. The result that had her name on the top and the date that marked the point where things had started to go so terribly wrong.

'I've got to go,' she cut Bella off. 'Just keep looking until you find it. Focus, Bella. It's not as if it's the first time you've dealt with this kind of thing and I really can't sit here and talk about it. I've got a lot on my plate right now.'

Too much. Kate hung up the phone, ignoring how hurt Bella's farewell had sounded after the brush-off. Her niece had no idea how lucky she was having a stupid piece of jewellery to worry about. Her own problem was a hell of a lot bigger.

Big enough to ruin her life.

Worse, it was big enough to ruin the life of the man she loved so much.

The house felt oddly empty.

Oliver checked his watch. Six-fifteen p.m. He wasn't late. He was home earlier than usual, in fact, because he'd promised to spend some time with his mother before attending an engagement on her behalf later this evening.

The event was the annual gala of her favourite children's charity and Oliver was going to present the main award on Lady Dorothy's behalf. She was anxious to make sure he knew exactly which people he couldn't omit spending time with, probably because they included members of the country's 'rich list' and were being groomed to become future sponsors.

But Lady Dorothy wasn't in her sitting room. Neither was Bella. Why was that so disappointing? Oh…that's right. Oliver had caught up with Wally's progress today and the chemotherapy her old patient was receiving seemed to be shrinking his brain tumour to the point where surgery might be possible without causing too much collateral damage. Bella would be thrilled to hear that. In fact, it had been Bella Oliver thought of instantly, when he'd been in the MRI lab scanning the latest results on Wally. He could imagine the joy dawning in her eyes and then spreading to the rest of her face and he knew it would culminate in one of those smiles that could light up the darkest of rooms. He couldn't deny that he was really looking forward to telling her the news.

But she wasn't there.

Oliver went swiftly back down the sweeping staircase and headed for the kitchen area. Yvonne, the housekeeper who came during the day, prepared meals amongst her other duties and left them in the kitchen. Bella was now in charge of reheating and serving his mother's dinner and Oliver knew she was also in the habit of eating with her employer now.

Unorthodox but perfectly acceptable when it gave him the freedom to stay at work for as long as was necessary without the worry of upsetting a routine that was more important than ever given his mother's health status. Oliver decided that was probably where they both were right now. Maybe his mother's blood sugar was a little lower than it should be after her evening dose of insulin so Bella had decided to serve dinner earlier than usual.

Except that the kitchen was also empty.

Very strange. Unsettling.

Oliver wandered from room to room on the main floor of the house, the silence pressing in on him and somehow making him more aware of the size of his family home than he'd ever been. It was huge by any standard. Ridiculous that only two people lived there.

Three, if you counted Bella, he supposed.

And who wouldn't count Bella? Oliver's mouth twisted into a wry smile. Given the size of Bella Graham's personality, she probably filled as much space as three ordinary people would.

The smile faded but Oliver found himself wishing for the faint strains of some foot-stomping country music to be coming from one of these vast, deserted spaces.

Like the drawing room. The library. The conservatory... Was his track taking him there automatically because he remembered the last time he had been in there? With the awful music and that glow of happiness and pride in his mother's face? And Bella, making the very air in this house feel like it had more oxygen or something in it?

There was nobody in the conservatory but there was a half-drunk cup of tea on a glass-topped table that was part of a suite of cane furniture screened by oversized potted palm trees. Beside the cup and saucer was a blood-glucose meter that still had a testing strip poking out of the end. Beside that lay an empty insulin syringe.

Oliver's breath left his chest in an exasperated huff. The syringe might have a needle that was small enough to be virtually invisible but it should have been put in a sharps container the instant it had been finished with.

Bella should know better.

Where the hell *was* she?

Raising his head as if to look for her, Oliver saw that the French doors of the conservatory were open and beyond them he could see a figure standing in the middle of the lawn. His mother, apparently caught by the shimmer of the sea in the soft light of dusk.

With a surge of relief, Oliver strode outside.

'Mother!' he called as he got closer. 'How are you?'

Lady Dorothy didn't answer. She didn't even turn her head.

'Where's Bella?' The inflection on the query faded as if Oliver didn't actually expect a response. Maybe he had instinctively known there wouldn't be one. He was still operating on autopilot, however, bending to kiss his mother's cheek. Well before his lips brushed her skin, he knew something was wrong.

Lady Dorothy was still staring out to sea, totally unaware of his presence. The lights were on but nobody was home and Oliver knew exactly what was happening. He didn't have to touch her skin to feel how clammy and cold it was. Or to pick up her wrist to feel the rapid pulse. His mother's blood sugar was dangerously low and she was only seconds away from losing consciousness completely.

And she was standing outside. By *herself.*

With a speed and control fuelled by fury, Oliver picked his mother up in his arms as if she weighed nothing and strode back into the house. Through the conservatory and back towards the kitchen, almost colliding with Bella as she came flying down the staircase.

'Oh, my God,' she gasped, the colour draining from her face. 'What's happened?'

Oliver kept going without saying a word, aware of Bella following because he could hear her breath hitch in a half-sob. Carefully, he put his mother down on a chair beside the kitchen table, pausing for a moment to check that she was still conscious enough to remain upright. Bella crouched beside the chair, her arms outstretched to offer support.

Lady Dorothy sat there in her robot-like state, apparently unaware of Bella's horrified face even though she was staring straight at her nurse.

'What's happened,' Oliver finally snapped as he headed for the fridge, 'is that you left my mother alone, *outside*, to have a hypoglycaemic attack.' He wrenched the fridge door open and jerked out the drawer that held the insulin supplies. Amongst all the preloaded syringes were some clear plastic sachets. He was ripping one open as he turned back to his mother.

'I'd only been gone for a couple of minutes.' Bella's voice was strained, her face as pale as his mother's was. 'Lady Dorothy thought of somewhere else her necklace might be…said I had to go and look right now in case she forgot later…'

Oliver ignored the flow of words that were obviously supposed to be excusing the inexcusable. He was rubbing the glucose gel from the sachet across his mother's gums and over her tongue. She could still swallow safely, thank goodness, but if it was necessary, he had the supplies available to administer intravenous glucose.

His anger hadn't faded at all yet.

'I have a job I have to go to, in case you hadn't noticed,' he told Bella. 'I can't be in two places at once so, unless I give up my position at St Patrick's, I can't take total responsibility for my mother's health care. That's what *you* were employed for and I thought you could be trusted.'

Bella wasn't saying anything. Oliver ignored the tiny sniffle he heard. Why did women seem to think that crying was going to fix anything? He glanced at his watch. If the glucose gel was going to work, it should be starting to have an effect by now.

He would call an ambulance if he had to, of course, but remembering how upset his mother had been the last time such a fuss had been made, it would be preferable to avoid such drastic measures.

And the glucose she was rapidly absorbing through her mucous membranes seemed to be working finally. He could feel the tone returning to her sagging body and saw her blinking her eyes.

'Oh…my…' Lady Dorothy's voice sounded surprisingly strong. 'Where am I?'

'In the kitchen,' Oliver said. 'You had a hypo, Mum.'

'Oh, dear. I'm sorry, darling.'

'There's no need for you to be sorry,' Oliver growled. 'It was hardly *your* fault.'

It was *her* fault.

Bella didn't need Oliver's barbed, indirect comment to hammer the guilt home.

She couldn't look at him either because she didn't want to see the look that told her how hopeless he thought she was.

'I'll go and get the glucometer,' she muttered, scrambling to her feet. They would need to check Lady Dorothy's blood-sugar level to be sure that whatever measures they were taking now were effective enough to ensure that her patient didn't lapse into a coma later tonight.

And die in her sleep.

No wonder Oliver was so furious with her. How stupid had it been to follow directions that had left Lady Dorothy on her own straight after an insulin injection? There were all sorts of reasons why a reaction could be stronger or more rapid than usual and the control of Lady Dorothy's diabetes had been noticeably more fragile since she'd become ill. If she'd been there, she might have heard the elderly woman's speech become slurred or noticed that her behaviour was unusual. Or seen the sheen of perspiration on pale skin.

Noticing that kind of change was precisely why Lady Dorothy needed a nurse with her and not just a companion who could encourage her to do her exercises and keep her spirits up while she coped with the aftermath of the episode of acute rheumatoid arthritis.

Even Kate had been annoyed with her that morning. Virtually accused her of being unable to focus. Scatterbrained. Always losing things.

Oliver was making a cheese sandwich for his mother by the time she got back to the kitchen. Lady Dorothy had clearly recovered.

'It was my own fault,' she was saying to her son. 'I sent Bella away to look for my necklace.'

'What necklace?'

'The lovely garent one, you know? You found it in a junk shop when you were about ten and gave it to me for my birthday.'

Bella cringed inwardly as she peeled open the foil packet containing a test strip and then fished a lancet from the kit. So the necklace had been a gift from Oliver? A sentimental treasure?

Her day was just going from bad to worse. She twisted the tiny plastic square from the base to expose the hidden pin of the lancet.

'Sorry, Lady Dorothy,' she murmured, reaching for a hand that still had painfully swollen joints. 'Small prick coming.'

The fact that the reading was within a normal range already failed to lift Bella's spirits.

'I'll have my dinner and then a bath,' Lady Dorothy declared. 'And then I'm going to watch all the episodes of *Coronation Street* that I've missed this week. You can have the night off, Bella. I'm sorry to have given you a fright, dear.'

Bella didn't meet the glare she could feel coming from Oliver's direction. 'I'll have to check your BGL every so often,' she said apologetically, 'but I'll try not to disturb you if you want an evening to yourself.'

'I do,' Lady Dorothy said firmly. 'I'm embarrassed that this happened. It won't happen again, I promise. Can I have my dinner now, please, Bella?'

'Of course.'

'Will you join me, Oliver?'

'I'll have to eat later, at the gala,' he said. 'And I'd like to get a workout in but I'm all yours for a while, Mother. Remind me who I need to be polite to tonight.'

Bella served dinner in the dining room but left Oliver alone with his mother. She wasn't hungry herself and she certainly didn't want to hang around. She ran a bath for Lady Dorothy and made sure the taped episodes of her favourite television programme were ready for her in her private sitting room. She checked Lady Dorothy's blood-sugar level again, ignoring the elderly woman's impatience with the procedure.

'I'll be back to do it again in an hour,' she warned.

Bella went to her own room but it felt like a prison. What was she doing here when she couldn't even do her job properly? When she couldn't even look after her patient's precious, sentimental piece of jewellery?

With nothing better to do and a determination to put at least one thing right today, Bella set off, tracing every single footstep she'd taken on the day the necklace had gone missing.

A path that led, inevitably, to the gymnasium with its swimming and spa pools.

It was just after eight p.m. and the last rays of a blood-red sunset were bathing the gymnasium in a glow that needed no artificial enhancement.

Bella hadn't expected the area to still be in use. OK, Oliver had said something about needing a workout before he went off to some glitzy function but that had been hours ago. Surely he'd had time to get himself exercised and cleaned up and drive off to meet up with whoever the woman was that she'd overheard Oliver mention when she'd been serving dinner?

Monique. The name sounded as posh as the charity ball or whatever it was. He'd 'arranged a suitable partner', Oliver had been telling his mother in response to an unheard query. He'd said it with a finality that had seemed like yet another rebuke in Bella's day. As if she might have been thinking he could have asked her.

As if!

Bella was on a different planet as far as the social circle the Dawsons moved in. Right now she could feel the space between herself and Oliver as clearly as if there was a solid glass panel in place. Maybe that was why she didn't run away when she saw that Oliver was still using the exercise machines in the gym. It felt safe to stop for a moment and stare through the invisible window.

He was wearing nothing more than boxer shorts, his back to where Bella stood, in the middle of a routine that involved holding a free weight in each hand. Squats and lunges and arm raises that made the muscles all over his body bulge and ripple and the sheen of sweat shine in the sunset glow from outside.

Bella was transfixed.

She had never, *ever*, seen a more glorious specimen of a male body. The strength in those muscles. The control of the hold in positions that had to be painful. The elegant grace with which he moved from one position to another. The attraction was enough to make Bella's knees feel weak. She actually leaned against the doorframe as desire like none she had ever experienced stole through her body. She knew she shouldn't be doing this but couldn't help herself.

It was no worse than a bit of fantasy about, say, a

movie star, was it? It was the realm she'd always allocated to Oliver Dawson and it wasn't as if she was going to do anything about it. He wouldn't have a clue. She was quite safe while he had his back to her and she would steal away before he could turn.

Just a few seconds more.

Bella had no idea she had been slowly licking her lips until she touched them with her fingers and found them wet.

Oliver could feel the burn in every muscle in his body but he wasn't going to stop. Not yet.

Not when he could see Bella reflected in that mirror through the open dressing-room door.

When he could see the way she was looking at his body.

Wanting him.

He should be used to women looking at him like that. Maybe not in quite such an obvious fashion but Bella probably had no idea he could see her so clearly and it was irresistible not to keep going a little longer because it was like eavesdropping on someone's thoughts.

The way she was leaning on the wall like that, so loose limbed and relaxed, her arms bare in that singlet top and her tight jeans moulding her hips—did she have any idea how attractive a picture she made?

And when she licked her lips and then touched them… Dear God…the flame of a reciprocal desire was well and truly ignited for Oliver.

Not that he was going to act on it, of course. That would be totally inappropriate, not only because she was being employed to care for his mother but because she was so totally unlike any woman he'd ever allowed into the inner circle of his life. Whoever said that a class system didn't exist in New Zealand had never been involved in the kind of social circle he would be a valued member of later this evening.

To choose to be with someone like Bella Graham would be a form of rebellion and he had never done rebellion, had he?

Was that what he'd been missing out on all these years? What had propelled him prematurely into middle age?

The sun was sinking rapidly now and the light was fading more with every passing second. Any moment and Bella would realise that his workout was over and that he'd turn around and she'd be busted. Any moment now and she would probably slip silently away. Exactly what she would do if she saw him start to turn around, too.

So Oliver didn't turn around. He spoke to the reflection he could see in the mirror.

'Was there something you wanted, Bella?'

Oh…*God*…

How long had Oliver known she was standing here? The embarrassment was excruciating.

'I…um…I'm looking for your mother's necklace. I think it must be somewhere in here.'

'Come in, then.' Oliver picked up a towel that had been draped over the handlebars of the treadmill. He mopped the sweat off his face and then the front of his chest. 'Don't mind me. I'm about to hit the shower.'

Bella tried not to watch Oliver towelling himself off.

Or think about him sluicing that body with soap and water in a nearby shower. She could have scuttled back upstairs but the determination to salvage something from her day included more than finding that necklace.

She forced herself to walk closer to Oliver. 'I'd like to apologise,' she said quietly. 'I'm absolutely appalled at what happened this evening. It won't happen again, I promise.'

She looked up then, hoping she could convey the genuine message that Oliver could trust her to care for his mother.

He seemed to get it. He nodded slowly. He stepped closer to Bella.

So close that her mouth went dry. He seemed to have stepped so close that any barriers between them, invisible or otherwise, had simply vanished.

He *knew*, she realised. Somehow, he knew exactly what she'd been thinking when she'd been standing there so absorbed in watching his body.

The thought should have been horrific except for the intensity with which Oliver was looking at her. The eye contact that went on…and on… The *interest* she could sense coming from him.

Was it remotely possible that he found her as attractive as she found him? Judging by the way the air seemed to be crackling in the space between them, Bella had to believe it was possible.

And more exciting than anything had ever been in her whole, entire life.

The subtle movement of her body was instinctive. She barely felt herself tilt forward in invitation but she was aware of her lips parting. Of her tongue coming out to moisten them because they felt so incredibly dry. And she could see the way Oliver's gaze dropped as he watched her tongue.

She wasn't sure what happened next. When she thought about it later, it was simply a blur of excitement intense enough to be blinding. One moment they were standing there with the air about to ignite and then she was in Oliver's arms, being kissed like she had never, ever been kissed in her life.

It was overwhelming. A solid mass of almost naked, *perfect* male body that was touching Bella with a hunger that made her feel like the most desirable female in existence. She could smell the heat that still came from his body after a punishing workout. She could feel the way his tongue moved against hers, withdrawing and then thrusting, stroking the fires of need for it to be the real thing instead of an imitation performed by their joined mouths and dancing tongues.

She could feel the slick of sweat on his lower back that made it so easy to slip her hands beneath the elastic of his shorts. Could feel the rock-hard evidence of his desire pressing into the part of her that wanted more. *More...*

She must have whispered the plea aloud because Oliver groaned.

'No condom,' he growled.

'I'm safe.' Bella's words came out in a gasp as she pressed herself closer and moved to close the gap that had appeared between their mouths. She was safe. She'd been through the routine screening offered to medical personnel at St Pat's. She'd never been exposed to a sexually transmitted or blood-borne disease.

Oliver's hands were moving. He was cupping her breast.

'You're on the Pill?'

'Oh…' His thumb was grazing her nipple and Bella's knees almost buckled. 'Oh…*yes*…'

He was undoing her jeans now and that meant he wasn't stopping. Thank God for that…

Somewhere in the back of Bella's head a warning bell was sounding. *He thinks you've said that you're on the Pill*, a small voice whispered.

Stop now. This is dangerous. You don't know what could happen. This is quite probably the *most irresponsible thing you've ever considered doing.*

Bella had had plenty of practice not listening to that little voice. Besides, she knew what *could* happen but what were the odds, really? Pretty darned small and… and she could go for a swim afterwards and that would probably wash any risk away. If that didn't work, didn't she have a dose of the morning-after pill tucked away from a time it hadn't been needed after all?

And…the risk would be worth it, wouldn't it? She might never have this opportunity again.

Oliver's hands were against bare skin now. Touching the very core of the blinding heat of her need.

'*Oh*…' Bella gasped again. She was touching him now, too. Could feel the velvet over steel that her body was desperate to enfold. The past was irrelevant. The future ceased to exist.

'*Now*…' Bella pleaded. 'Oliver…*please*…now…'

CHAPTER SEVEN

WHAT *had* he been thinking?

Oliver Dawson found himself fumbling uselessly with his gold cufflinks. He *hadn't* been thinking, pure and simple. For the first time in his life, he'd been carried away by the moment. By something as base as physical desire. Even now, when he had come to his senses and realised how incredibly stupid he'd been, his body was betraying him with a stab of remembered pleasure. Of longing.

The knowledge that he wanted *more*.

It was about more than sex, he realised. That sense of freedom he'd experienced giving in to the temptation to do something because it was what he wanted for himself had been irresistible.

Intoxicating.

The worst thing about it was that he had been perfectly well aware of exactly how much of a risk he was taking. It was, without doubt, the first *real* risk with potentially catastrophic consequences that he'd ever taken in his life.

It was certainly the first time he'd ever had unprotected sex.

Oh…*God*… He groaned aloud, following the sound

with a muttered oath as he jerked his dinner suit off the clothes hanger.

He had to walk past the gymnasium as he left his bedroom suite but it felt like only minutes since he'd been in there with Bella. Hell, it had only been a matter of minutes. At least the alarm sounding on his watch to remind him of his obligations elsewhere had been an excuse to escape having to deal with the aftermath of what he'd done in front of Bella.

He couldn't just leave things like that, though, could he? Bella might think it had been the start of…something. She might say something, even, in front of his mother.

Was she still in there? As he'd rushed off to have a shower and get changed she'd said something about having a quick swim before going back to check on Lady Dorothy.

Yes. Wrapped in a towel, Bella seemed to be lying on the floor of the gymnasium, her limbs jerking in a fashion that made alarm bells ring for Oliver. He was beside her in seconds.

'What's wrong?'

'N-nothing…' Bella wriggled, pulling her arm out from beneath the treadmill. She scrambled to her feet, the movement loosening the towel and giving Oliver an unwanted glimpse of her still naked body.

And he'd thought that shaft of renewed desire he'd had moments earlier was as much as he'd have to resist from now on?

He'd been dreaming. This was going to be torture. Oliver sucked in a steadying breath. He had to gain control here. Better late than never.

'That…what happened here…it shouldn't have happened, Bella.'

She was eyeing his dinner suit and Oliver suddenly felt ridiculously overdressed in his Armani suit and velvet bow-tie.

'You're employed by my mother,' he continued.

It was a good enough reason to excuse himself from the almost palpable awareness that what had happened here might possibly happen again. No, make that probably happen again. And again.

He simply couldn't let that happen.

Not after a lifetime of doing the right thing. Doing what he was supposed to do. Oliver wasn't about to fall off the rails on a regular basis. Tasting the freedom of pleasing only himself was intoxicating enough but the lure of doing it again was dangerous. Self-indulgence could only undermine what his life had been about for as long as he could remember.

It could turn him into the kind of person his father had been.

He had made his own rules and learned how to earn self-respect, if nothing else.

'It can't happen again,' he heard himself say, his voice curiously raw. 'It's just not…appropriate.'

'No-o-o…' Bella's smile was crooked. She gave his suit another glance and then looked over her shoulder, taking in their surroundings. 'Bit like bonking one of the servants, really, wasn't it?'

Oliver's jaw dropped. 'That's a ridiculous thing to suggest.'

'Is it?' Bella fiddled with the towel again, tucking it

more firmly around her body. As she did so, something came loose from her hand.

'What's that?' The query came out as a snap because Oliver realised he was angry at her inference that he'd taken advantage as someone in a more powerful position than she was. Or that she was in some way socially inferior. That wasn't the reason it was inappropriate at all. It was because she was his mother's nurse. Or maybe that wasn't the *real* reason either. Bella was so totally the opposite of anyone he'd ever been remotely attracted to. So carefree and full of life and...well, just...*Bella*. The way she was right now, with her face lighting up with a smile.

She personified rebellion, that's what it was. And while the attraction was undeniable, could there be a space in his life for something like that on a regular basis?

Oliver could feel a hard, grim band curling around inside his gut and it tightened with a painful jerk. Of course there wasn't.

Bella held out her hand to show him the object and Oliver recognised the necklace he'd given his mother so many years ago.

'It was under the treadmill,' Bella told him delightedly. 'I spotted it when I was...when we were... Anyway, I kind of forgot but then remembered when I was swimming.'

Oliver could feel his eyebrows rising. She'd been distracted by the glint of jewellery in the middle of the most mind-blowing sex he'd ever experienced?

Bella seemed to be watching him carefully. 'Afterwards,' she said softly. 'Not *during*...' Her smile widened. 'That's a ridiculous thing to suggest.'

She'd made him laugh.

Funnily enough, it had been that genuinely amused, appreciative sound that that provided the tipping point for Bella.

You'd think it was the raw power that came from a man with his kind of intelligence and status that would have done it.

Or the sheer physical beauty, not only of his body but in the way he made love.

But no. It was a chuckle. A moment of connection that touched something so different in Bella's soul, she knew she was lost.

Head over heels in love with Oliver Dawson.

Or should that be hopelessly in love?

Yep. That was the one because nothing could ever come of it. Bella was doomed to live with the agony of unrequited passion.

That became painfully obvious the next morning, after a sleepless night of vacillating between the pleasure of reliving every moment beside the pool to the pain of seeing Oliver looking so impossibly gorgeous in that dinner suit, heading off to spend the rest of his evening in the company of appropriate people. Appropriate *women*. Like that Monique.

He came into Lady Dorothy's suite to say goodbye and wish his mother a good day—the way he did most mornings.

Bella was helping Lady Dorothy to apply the minimum of make-up that she deemed necessary even for a day when they wouldn't be leaving the house. Thank goodness she was putting the lid back on the lipstick and not applying it to Lady Dorothy's face when her hand shook that little bit.

He did speak to her as he left.

'Have a good day, Bella,' he had said.

The eye contact had been brief enough that the knowledge that Oliver was deliberately avoiding any kind of connection was unmistakable. Bella had primed herself to be ready for it but it was still crushing.

Unbearable.

Or was it?

Maybe she deserved the rejection because she'd done the most irresponsible thing ever. Told the biggest lie ever. Maybe Oliver knew instinctively that she wasn't trustworthy. She could hardly reassure him now and tell him that she'd taken that morning-after pill. She hadn't been that reassured herself when she'd noticed it was past its expiry date but, hey...they built in a huge safety margin, didn't they?

Bella went on with the routine of the day in an uncharacteristically subdued manner. She checked Lady Dorothy's blood-sugar levels and administered her insulin, quickly followed by a robust breakfast of scrambled eggs and parsley on toast. She made sure that she recorded everything in the notes she was keeping on her patient, adding in a few extras as well, like blood pressure, heart rate and respiration rate measurements. A neatly written paragraph about the progress Lady Dorothy was making filled up the whole page of the big diary for that day. A diary she knew that Oliver would be checking more carefully after yesterday's hypogly-caemic episode.

A large part of the afternoon was taken up with ex-amining a catalogue from a medical supplies firm and discussing the merits of various assistive devices with Lady Dorothy.

'I think the easy-grip cutlery would be worth a try. And the high-lipped plates.'

'Baby stuff,' Lady Dorothy sniffed. 'I'm getting bet-ter at feeding myself, aren't I?'

'Yes, but with that high edge on the plate you could chase your food until you caught it. You wouldn't need me to put it on the spoon. And, you never know, that dinky little knife might mean you could cut things up yourself, too. You wouldn't need me to do anything. Independence isn't babyish.' Bella threw in a trump card. 'Nanna would have loved these. She hated being fed.'

'We could give them a try, I suppose,' Lady Dorothy conceded. 'And maybe you're right about that shower chair. I'd like to be able to do that by myself too.'

'At the rate you're going, they'll probably be tempo-rary aids. Think of them like using crutches for a bro-ken ankle or something.'

'Hmm. In that case, let's have another look at that modified keyboard thing. I'm missing doing my emails.'

Bella was already filling in an order form. 'If I ring the supplier, they might be able to deliver it all by to-morrow. Later today even.'

'Don't forget we're doing the spa pool again later.'

Bella's smile was forced. Having to be back in that space with its new memories was something she might well try to avoid but she was hardly likely to forget because she knew how hard it would be.

And it was. But in the turmoil of thoughts and feelings that even walking past the treadmill engendered, something happened to move her forward a step. A new notion presented itself and it grew slowly over the next day or two, especially when Oliver relaxed a little as the normal routine of his life was re-established, uninterrupted by any challenge from Bella to revisit their impulsive connection. When he could actually meet Bella's gaze and exchange more than a few words with her, as though nothing untoward had even happened.

He'd sounded almost pleased to be talking to her today, in fact, when he'd been telling her about Wally's surgery and how well it had gone. The elderly man hadn't regained consciousness yet so they couldn't know whether there would be any lasting effects but, at the moment, things were looking good and they may well have given him a good few extra years.

Bella had been thrilled to hear the news, of course. So thrilled that her plan took final shape and was clearly the way forward for her because it meant she would be able to retain her pride. With a bit of luck, it might mean those little cracks in her heart from the pressure of unrequited love might heal as well.

The plan was centred on the fact that Bella was doing an exceptionally good job with Lady Dorothy. Oliver would notice her record-keeping. He would notice the progress his mother was making over the next while, too. Progress that could well speed up with the arrival of all those assistive devices that had been ordered with no expense spared.

Bella had no doubt that she could earn Oliver's professional respect and, more importantly, his *trust* by doing her job so well she would also be showing him that she wasn't about to run away from a challenge. Or the humiliation of knowing that she wasn't *appropriate*.

Maybe that was because it wasn't that humiliating. Bella knew perfectly well that there was no way she would ever fit into the Dawson world—but he'd proved she wasn't undesirable and that more than made up for it. In a way, it gave her the power to control the feelings she had for Oliver.

Yes, they were inappropriate and couldn't go anywhere but there was no doubt that they added a most delicious sexual frisson in the atmosphere every time Oliver was in the same room as she was. It was there faintly from simply being in his house and while it was frustrating, it wasn't unpleasant. A bit like window shopping, perhaps, when you allowed yourself the pleasure of imagining that you were going to win the lottery soon and could actually buy anything you wanted.

Last night had been the clincher. Oliver had come out into the garden to visit his mother and Bella had excused herself to give them some time alone together. Had it been deliberate to squeeze through the gap between the chairs so close to where Oliver was preparing to sit down?

She'd been close enough to hear the way he sucked his breath in, anyway. And she had *felt* the way his gaze had followed her back to the house. She'd felt it all the way down to her bones. Bella had stopped just inside the French doors of the conservatory and taken a backwards glance, just in time to see him turning his head towards his mother.

But she *knew*. Oliver was feeling the same sexual tension that she was.

He couldn't avoid her completely because she spent so much time with his mother. He couldn't fire her because she was employed by Lady Dorothy and, anyway, why would he fire someone who was helping his beloved mother so much?

There was something else he couldn't do anything about either, and that was if Bella teased him with that new awareness.

Just a little. Just enough to make sure they *both* knew what it was they really wanted.

She might not be appropriate and Oliver might be quite right in thinking he didn't want her in his life on a permanent basis but he wanted her now and when she left in a few months' time Bella had a new determination to make sure that he realised what he'd missed out on.

Getting away to Australia for a few days to attend a conference in Melbourne had been the best idea Oliver had had for some time.

Professionally, it was stimulating. Personally, it gave him the space to deal with the uncomfortable blip in his life that his encounter with Bella had caused.

That upheaval in his private life was more than two weeks ago now. Clearly his mother had no idea that anything untoward had occurred between her son and her private nurse and life had returned to sit within its normal, albeit new, parameters. Oliver was quite confident that he could go back to doing the best job he was capable of at St Patrick's, ensure that his mother was as comfortable and happy as possible and keep up his social obligations when it came to the charity work that was synonymous with the Dawson family name.

That confidence was still with him when he arrived home that evening from the airport. He found his mother in her study and Oliver's confidence went up a notch when he saw what she was doing.

The modified keyboard had been a brilliant idea of Bella's. The motivation to keep up with old friends and current events had seen his mother overcome the initial challenge of the movement her hands and fingers were required to make. Thanks to Bella's encouragement, she had persevered to the point where the contact with the outside world was so enjoyable that the exercise was proving very beneficial and her range of movements seemed to be increasing daily.

'Lovely to see you home, darling,' Lady Dorothy said. 'But I'm awfully busy getting the organisation for this new fundraiser under way. I gave Bella the night off so I could get on with it. Maybe we could have breakfast together?'

Oliver went off to unpack his bag with a smile on his face. Things were all as they should be at home. Better, even. No doubt about it. Bella was doing an exemplary job as Lady Dorothy's private nurse and there had been no more incidents with the diabetes control. Oliver had kept a tight watch on things up until he'd taken the risk of going away for a few days but everything had run just as smoothly at home while he'd been away. Finally, he knew he could relax and trust Bella to look after his mother.

He could trust her not to say anything about what had happened that night, too, and that was a biggie. It wasn't that his mother would have been appalled, she was far too open-minded for that. Quite the opposite would have happened, Oliver suspected, and he would find all sorts of cunning plans put in motion that would leave him alone with Bella.

And it had been hard enough to be in her company even when they weren't alone. For those first few days he'd been acutely aware of everything about her. So aware he could have sworn he could smell her hair from the other side of a room. He could certainly taste her kisses when he awoke alone at night after some of the most erotic dreams he'd had since his teenage years.

He'd proved he could handle it, however, and this new level of confidence made him think he was over the worst. He'd probably be able to spend time with Bella without even thinking of ripping her clothes off.

The confidence lasted until he went downstairs to his own suite. It lasted precisely a heartbeat as he walked past the open door of the gymnasium and saw Bella climbing out of the swimming pool.

Water was cascading off every inch of her gorgeous, golden-brown skin. The tiny bikini she wore might as well have been invisible for the effect it had on Oliver's body. He should keep moving and remove himself from the sight as soon as possible but his feet were refusing to comply. His chest seemed to be having trouble following even a subconscious directive to breathe.

Reaching for a towel that was draped over the hand rail at the top of the steps, Bella looked up and saw him.

'Oh…God…sorry!' she exclaimed. 'I thought you were still in Melbourne.'

'No.' Oliver's throat felt like sandpaper. He cleared it. 'I'm back,' he said.

Bella grinned. 'So you are.'

Oliver's reaction to the teasing about his redundant statement was an odd mix of annoyance and…delight? Who else in his life teased him the way Bella did?

She was wrapping the towel around herself. Coming towards him.

'I'll get out of your way,' she said. 'I can have a shower in my own room.'

She was so close now Oliver could feel her warmth. A steamy, damp kind of warmth that made him think of sex.

God…Bella always made him think of sex.

He had to fight to make sure his hands stayed by his sides and didn't reach for Bella as she went past him in the doorway. It would have been so easy to touch her. Just a soft brush on her arm maybe. And she would stop and look at him and…and there would be no going back.

Oliver pulled in some oxygen to try and kick-start his brain. *Move*, it ordered. *Now*. It was like that moment before that first kiss all over again.

There was space between their bodies but the air was crackling with such intensity that they might as well have been skin to skin.

Bella could feel the heat melting her bones. Like an out-of-body experience she could almost see herself slowing down. If she paused for just a moment, whatever it was in the air would ignite and she would find herself in his arms again without being aware of quite how it had happened.

Except…Oliver was moving away from her. Towards the rooms that were even more of a private sanctuary than the gymnasium. The bedroom Bella had never been invited into.

OK, she'd had a peek in there while he was away. Stood in the doorway of the vast bedroom that had a bay window with the same gorgeous view of the ocean that the best rooms in the rest of the house had. The sight of the vast bed with its masculine, burgundy cover had made her pulse skip a beat and Bella had been very tempted to go and bury her face in one of the pillows to see if she could catch a hint of Oliver. The scent of his skin, maybe, which she would recognise instantly.

Bella kept moving herself as well. Heading for *her* own room upstairs because dealing with moments like that in a mature and responsible fashion was part of behaving herself with the most decorum she had available. Sticking to her plan and obeying all the new rules that came with it. Making up for the most irresponsible lapse she'd ever had.

She'd taken that morning-after pill. She still had the pregnancy test kit that had come with it, along with the instructions to use it three weeks after taking the pill. Just in case.

It was nearly three weeks now, wasn't it?

If Bella went and got that responsibility out of the way, it was possible she could relax a bit more. Maybe even bend the new rules so that things might work out a little differently if another opportunity presented itself like the one that still seemed to be exerting a magnetic pull that made her want to do a U-turn and tap on Oliver's door. The longing was overwhelmingly powerful. Forbidden and delicious, and Bella knew she would be feeling its subtle aftershocks for hours. Probably for the rest of the night.

But a remarkably short time later the memory of that sexually charged moment had been completely obliterated and the aftershocks Bella was experiencing were very, very different.

And definitely very unpleasant.

Horrific even.

Shortly after that, Bella slipped out of the Dawsons' house. There was only one place she could think of being when life threw this kind of a curve ball at her. Only one person she needed to be with.

Kate.

CHAPTER EIGHT

'You're *what*?'

Bella closed her eyes. Something was going wrong here. She didn't know quite how she'd expected Kate to react to the news but she hadn't pictured this. The way her aunt had gone as white as a sheet. To look as though…as though Bella had *stabbed* her in the heart or something.

'I'm pregnant,' she said for the second time. A whisper now.

'*Bella*. How *could* you?'

They were standing in the kitchen of Kate's house because she'd been cooking. Connor was running late, apparently. Bella was welcome to stay and have dinner with them both. Or she had been, until she'd summoned her courage and blurted out the frightening results of that damned test.

'It was an accident.'

Kate's snort was contemptuous. 'So that makes everything all right? For God's sake, Bella. You're twenty-six. You *know* about contraception.'

'It just…happened.' Oh, God…that sounded *so* pathetic. How many times had Bella heard other people make an excuse like that and thought how stupid they were? No wonder Kate was looking so incredibly angry.

'No, it didn't,' she snapped. 'It was you being totally irresponsible. *Again.*'

Bella's heart sank even further. She'd come here for help. She didn't need a lecture. She needed advice. From the person she was closest to in the world. An aunt who was more like a sister. A best friend.

Something was bubbling away in a pot on the stove behind Kate. A pasta sauce, probably. The aroma of garlic and oregano should have been delicious but Bella was aware of faint nausea. The first physical symptoms of her pregnancy, or was it fear that she'd really gone too far this time and even Kate wasn't going to be prepared to help her pick up the pieces of the latest disaster she'd created?

Kate seemed to have forgotten the pot. She moved her arms and it looked as if she was hugging herself. Instead of Bella. Yes…that's the reaction she had expected. Desperately wanted.

'Who's the father?' Kate's voice was hollow. It was an automatic question. A way of filling a horrible silence.

'Oliver Dawson.'

There was another silence as Kate absorbed what was clearly a shock.

'Does he know?'

'Of course not. I only found out myself five minutes ago. I've got no intention of telling him either.'

Kate's breath came out in an incredulous huff. 'You don't think he might notice?'

'He doesn't have to.' She could leave. Go somewhere

else to have her baby. Her mother would help her if Kate wouldn't but it was Kate she wanted to have on her side. To help her tell her mother, if nothing else.

Kate was staring at her now. She was actually shaking.

'Don't you dare… Don't even think about it.'

'About what?' What was so wrong in keeping a father out of the picture? Millions of women did it. OK, it wasn't ideal but it wasn't a hanging offence, was it?

'Getting rid of it,' Kate said hoarsely. 'You can't. You mustn't…'

It was Bella's turn to stare now. She'd never seen Kate look like this. Ever. Her face seemed to be dissolving. Moving into lines of…grief?

'It would haunt you for ever,' Kate said. 'You'd think about it every time you saw a baby. Every time it was the day that should have been its birthday. You'd think about how old it would be and whether it would be walking yet or talking…or if it might look like that kid you just saw in someone else's pram…'

Whatever it was in the pot was burning now. Bella could smell it but she couldn't say anything. The way Kate was looking was unbearable. The way she was dragging her breath in as though it was physically painful.

'Did you…have you had an abortion?' Bella whispered.

'No…' Kate's voice rose in her vehemence. 'And I'm not going to. I just *can't…*'

'You don't need to.' Bella shook her head. This was surreal. '*I'm* the one who's pregnant.'

'You don't get it.' Kate was shouting now. Calm, controlled Kate who never shouted. Who certainly never looked like this. 'You're not the only one who's pregnant.'

'Oh…my God… Kate, you're *pregnant*?'

The words were inside Bella's head, but they hadn't come out of her mouth. Both Bella and Kate turned towards the door. Connor was standing there, looking just as pale as Kate had when Bella had told her why she'd come.

Kate made an agonised sound. 'I'm sorry,' she said brokenly. 'I'm so sorry…' And then she turned and fled.

Bella couldn't move. She stared at Connor. Connor stared back. He still looked pale and there was no expression on his face whatsoever. He looked…cold. Angry? Maybe. Terrifying? Definitely.

'Turn that pot off, will you?' Connor said quietly a long, long moment later. 'Before the house burns down?' And then he turned as well and went after Kate.

Poor Kate, Bella thought. Oh, my God. Bella turned off the scorched sauce. She didn't know what to do next because her world was falling down around her ears. So *this* was what had been bothering Kate so much. Why she wasn't so excited about the wedding. Neither of them wanted children. Was this a deal-breaker?

No. Please, no. Bella sank into a chair beside the kitchen table and buried her face in her hands. For some inexplicable reason it felt like this was all her fault.

'I'm sorry, Connor.' Kate's heart was breaking. She could actually feel it splintering, the shards stabbing in her chest as she stood there in the garden and Connor came up behind her and enfolded her in his arms.

She very badly wanted to turn into him and bury her face against his chest and give in to the pain that wanted to escape in gut-wrenching sobs but Kate fought the urge. The battle was enough to make her tremble from head to foot.

'I know it's the very last thing you want.' Her voice was trembling, too. 'That you never want a child of your own because of Pippi.'

She drew in a shuddering breath as she felt the pressure of Connor's arms turning her towards him. Pippi had been the baby of Connor's family. The longed-for girl who had become sick with leukaemia and eventually died, fragmenting the family. The determination not to let history repeat had been born then for Connor even if he hadn't realised it. What had he told her that time? That kids were a potential bomb waiting to go off and destroy a whole family. That it was a risk he was never going to take.

Connor had been a lost little boy. Forgotten and left to feel abandoned and unloved. Kate knew what that felt like and the connection had been so powerful that hearing his story had been the moment she had realised how much she loved him. She wanted to hold him close and show him how much he *was* loved.

Incredibly, such a short time ago, it had seemed like she had her whole life to show him that love. But now she was pregnant and he wouldn't want to cope with that. Maybe he wasn't capable of coping and the challenge would be too much. It would send him away.

Kate had her face against Connor's chest now. 'I know it should be easy to…to *fix* things,' she said shakily, 'but I can't and I can't even tell you *why* because…'

The trembling in her body intensified to become shaking. Connor's arms tightened around her and somehow he moved them so that Kate found herself sitting beside him but she couldn't look up at him because she was too scared of what she might see in his face.

He put his fingers under her chin, though, and lifted her face, and what she saw there wasn't anger or rejection. It was…it was far more heartbreaking. He looked so sad.

'Never say that, Katie,' he said. 'You can tell me anything.' He touched her face gently. 'I know that bad stuff happened to you. How could I not? You remember the first time we tried to make love?'

Of course she did. It had been a disaster.

'That bad stuff—you getting raped by your so-called boyfriend—was in the way.'

'In the way' was an understatement. It had seemed to spell the end of a potential relationship. Kind of like the way this pregnancy was spelling doom for their impending marriage.

'You still don't know everything,' Kate said, her voice breaking as she pulled her hand away from Connor's.

'So tell me,' was all Connor said quietly.

Kate swallowed hard. 'There were…repercussions from the rape.'

Connor went very, very still. 'You got *pregnant*?' She heard the sharp sound of his indrawn breath. 'You had an abortion?'

That would explain why she was so upset about Bella's plan to 'fix' things, wouldn't it? But he still didn't understand. It was worse than that.

'I didn't try to find a way out,' she said softly. 'I didn't even tell anyone. I…I wanted that baby *so* much, Connor. It would have been someone to love. Someone who would…' Her voice was almost inaudible. 'Who would have loved me back.'

Connor's voice was raw. 'What happened?'

'I was a bit over five months pregnant, I guess, and I got careless. My father saw me coming out of the bathroom in the T-shirt I slept in and he was so angry.'

Connor made a growling sound. 'He hit you?'

'He didn't get a chance. I ran. I got as far as the front door but then I tripped on the step and fell…hard.' There was no point going into the gory details. 'I lost the baby,' she finished quietly. 'And that was when Mum shipped me off to my brother's. I was sixteen.'

There was a long silence. Then Connor took hold of her hand again and she could hear the hint of a smile in his voice.

'Do you remember when we *did* get to make love?'

Kate nodded. Of course she did. How could she ever forget? It had been in her office, no less. After he had saved her from her father's violent attack.

'Why did it work that time?'

'Because…I felt safe.'

'But why did you feel safe?'

'Because I loved you and…and that was when I found out that you loved *me*.' The miracle of it was still fresh. Kate could hear the wonder in her voice.

'Mmm.' Connor was stroking his thumb across the back of her hand. 'It got you past that barrier, didn't it? Feeling loved. Feeling safe?'

'Mmm.'

'Well, my barrier was the thought of having a child with the potential for something to go horribly wrong and for it to destroy a family. Looking at it now, I think it was all to do with the loneliness of feeling abandoned. Being vulnerable.'

Kate had to touch Connor. To connect with him in a way that words couldn't hope to convey. She reached up to touch his face. To trace the outline of his eyes and his cheekbones and his jaw. She wanted him to know that she understood. That she loved him. That he would never, ever be abandoned again.

Connor smiled down at her. He caught her hand with his own. 'I don't feel like that any more.'

'You mean...' Kate wasn't sure exactly what he meant because what she wanted it to mean was too much to hope for.

'The biggest risk I ever took was loving you, Katie,' he said softly. 'And it was a risk I had no choice but to take because I *do* love you. And you love me. And I feel safe, too. Kids don't seem like that big a risk any more.'

He was smiling at her now. A slightly wobbly smile but it was full of joy. 'We can do anything, Katie, my love. Nothing's going to destroy our love and to have a baby...*our* baby, maybe *lots* of babies...it's only going to make that love bigger, don't you think? Stronger, anyway.'

'But what if something goes wrong? Like Pippi?'

'We'll have each other. We'd be strong for each other. And we'd know not to forget to show that love to each other. And to our children.'

'Oh, Connor...' Kate threw her arms around the man

she loved and he held her just as tightly. 'I love you *so* much. You're going to be the *best* father.'

'And you're going to be a totally awesome mum. You've even had practice with teenagers.'

'Oh, no…' Kate pulled reluctantly out of Connor's embrace. '*Bella.*'

Connor sighed. 'I think she might need you right now even more than I do. What are you going to tell her?'

'I really don't know,' Kate confessed. 'It's a mess. The father of this baby is Oliver Dawson.'

'*Whoa…*' Connor was practically gaping at her. 'Does he know?'

'Apparently not.'

Connor shook his head. He watched Kate get to her feet to head back into the house.

'Want me to come in too?'

'Not yet. Bella and I have some talking to do. I think it's time she heard my whole story. And then we'll talk about what comes next.'

Connor watched her walk back into the house.

Pride filled his chest until it was so tight it was hard to breathe. No wonder he loved this woman so much. She was so strong. She'd been through so much. Being loved by her made him the luckiest man alive. And now she was carrying his baby.

His *baby*.

A grin came from nowhere and stayed on his face for a very long time. Finally, it faded into a somewhat rueful smile as he thought about Bella's predicament. About what Oliver Dawson was going to have to deal with.

Bella was another one of those strong Graham women. And a much wilder one than his Katie.

He could understand perfectly well why Oliver had been attracted to Bella but for the life of him he couldn't imagine Oliver seeing her as the chosen mother of his child. Even with his peers, the surgeon came across as being a bit pompous sometimes. Stuffy, even.

Man, but he'd love to be a fly on the wall when he got the news that Bella was carrying the Dawson heir.

And that thought was enough to propel Connor to his feet and into the house. They'd had plenty of time to talk and he had to make sure that Kate started looking after herself. Here it was after eight p.m. and he knew she hadn't had a bite of dinner yet. He didn't want Bella upsetting her either. Besides, Bella was part of *his* family now. They would find a way through this mess.

Together.

CHAPTER NINE

SOMETHING wasn't quite right.

Oliver couldn't put his finger on what it was but it was bothering him. His registrar gave him a sideways glance as they stood in front of the CT scan they were examining.

'Problem?'

Oliver gave his head a definitive shake. 'Looks straightforward to me. Burr holes here and here…' He indicated the spots. 'Lifting the bone flap over this area should give us clear access to the clot.'

'OK. I'll go and get scrubbed.' But the registrar gave him another odd glance, as if he could tell that something was bothering Oliver.

And it was, but it wasn't anything to do with any of the cases that were lined up for neurosurgery today.

It was Bella who kept sneaking into his head. He could banish her, of course, and get on with his job but she kept coming back. Leaving this odd, unsettled feeling behind.

Ever since he'd got back from Melbourne a week ago, since he'd come so close to kissing her again when she'd been walking past wrapped in that towel and looking so deliciously damp, she'd been…different. Not that he'd seen that much of her. Some days he didn't see her at all, in fact, and despite the plausible reasons his mother offered, he was beginning to think she was deliberately avoiding his company. And when he did see her, she was most definitely quieter.

Subdued, almost. More grown up or something.

And, as ridiculous as it the word seemed when describing Bella Graham, she seemed more *dignified.*

He hadn't heard her singing. Or laughing, come to think of it. He certainly hadn't seen her dancing.

Boyfriend hassles, perhaps?

Not that it was any of his business. And he certainly had no right to feel put out by the notion that there were other men in Bella's life.

Other men?

Good grief, where had that come from? As if *he* was in Bella's life.

Oliver scrubbed in with his usual attention to detail. A short time later, gowned and gloved, he supervised his registrar making the burr holes in the shaved area of their patient's head. It wasn't until the bone flap had been lifted and the dura exposed that he held his hand out for the surgical scissors required to snip through the protective covering of the brain.

For a good while then not a single thought of Bella intruded. The clot that had been pressing on this woman's brain after the head injury she'd sustained in a car accident was carefully extracted. There was no new bleeding to be seen and closing the wound was uneventful. The registrar was left with the task of replacing the bone flap and stitching the scalp back together. With her head swathed in bandages, the woman would go back to the ICU for observation and Oliver could check in on her before they started their next case. Stripping his gloves off as he left Theatre, he gave his mask a tug but only the top string broke, leaving it dangling around his neck.

Like a bib.

Like Bella's had been that day he'd growled at her for coming into his theatre in such slap-dash fashion.

And there she was again.

OK, it was his business if she had boyfriend issues that were making her unhappy. What if it wasn't a boyfriend? What if she was becoming bored with her new job of being his mother's private nurse?

That was a real possibility, wasn't it?

Bella was made for adventure. For doing wild, irresponsible things that involved lots of noise and movement and laughter. She might be doing an astonishing good job of helping his mother in her rehabilitation but how long could such a confined routine appeal to a free spirit like Bella?

She might decide to leave and head off on that overseas trip she was so keen on having and where would that leave his mother? And him?

This time, that unsettled feeling contained an extra element. Guilt. For some reason Oliver couldn't help thinking that he might be to blame for whatever was going on.

That attraction between them was as strong as it had been the night he'd totally lost control and given in to temptation. Maybe it was even stronger on his side judging by the pull he'd felt to kiss her again the other night. Was it the same for Bella? Was she feeling…rejected in some way, because he'd told her that it wasn't appropriate?

A bit like bonking one of the servants.

How absurd was that?

That hadn't been why it was so inappropriate. It had been because she was his mother's employee and even that wasn't enough of a reason in itself.

It was because she was who she was, it was as simple as that. Someone who could float through life in a joyous and carefree manner, flouting the rules if she thought she could get away with it or if it was going to be so much fun it would be worth it. She had no weight of social responsibilities or even the pressures of doing a high-powered job.

Oliver could feel the scowl on his face deepening as he strode off to do a quick ward round between theatre cases.

A knot of something like resentment was forming in his gut. Was he jealous of the kind of freedom Bella had?

No, of course he wasn't.

The social obligations were just a distraction. He didn't care about the status that went with being in an elite group of moneyed people but he did care about the power they had to change things in society that weren't right.

He did, however, love his job. He wouldn't swap it for anything. He loved the drama and pressure of Theatre and he got enormous satisfaction out of changing people's lives for the better. Stepping in when they—or their loved ones—were so terrified because something bad was happening inside a brain. The idea of the soul being located in the heart was so off beam. Everything happened inside the brain and if it got too damaged the person was lost for ever.

Like poor old Wally, who he was popping in to see now. The elderly gentleman who'd finally had his brain tumour removed was now back in the geriatric ward.

Oliver checked in with the nurse manager to see how he was doing.

'Not bad at all,' Sally told him. 'That left-sided weakness is still there but his speech is getting clearer every day. And once he relearns a word for something, it's there the next time he wants it.' She grinned. 'He's feeling so much better today he asked when the next line-dancing class was happening. He's missing Bella.'

Oliver just stared at Sally. That's what it was. *He* was missing Bella, too. The happy Bella. That's why he kept thinking about her at inappropriate moments. Why he was left feeling unsettled.

'We're all missing her,' Sally sighed, disconcertingly seeming to read his mind. 'She just has a knack of making the world around her a brighter place, doesn't she?'

Not right now she didn't.

'How's Lady Dorothy getting on?'

'Excellent progress,' Oliver reported. 'She can't manage her blood-sugar testing or her insulin injections by herself yet but she's getting more independent with other things every day. I think she'll end up needing very little assistance.'

'That's fantastic.' Sally raised her eyebrows. 'Maybe she won't need Bella much longer and we could have her back.'

'Doubt it. My mother has become very fond of Bella.' Oliver could feel his scowl trying to emerge again.

'Besides, she's planning to head overseas to have adventures as soon as she's not needed in this position.'

'Oh, that's right. The big O.E. and then settling down to have a dozen babies.' Sally laughed. 'Our Bella certainly knows what she wants out of life.'

Oliver said nothing. He was, to outward appearances, now deeply focussed on Wally's notes. What he was actually doing was breathing a sigh of relief. That was precisely why a relationship with Bella was so out of the question. It wasn't that she was so unlike the women he'd always dated because, right now, in this quiet, dignified mode, she wasn't that different after all. It was because she wanted something so different from her life. The kind of women he dated and that his mother was expecting him to choose from to produce a Dawson heir one day would have one or two children at the most. And a nanny to look after them, no doubt.

He could just see Bella with a dozen kids and no nanny. A whole, shambolic house full of them, tumbling around and dancing. And singing and shouting and laughing.

It would be loud and chaotic and…well… Oliver couldn't imagine any neurosurgeon who'd want to go home after a hard day's work to something like that.

He loved going home to the peace and quiet routine of his life. To the physical release of his gymnasium and the emotional peace of the summer house. He'd found it disruptive getting used to having Bella around in the first place. He should be delighted that her exuberance was wearing off and things were getting back to more like they had been in the past.

As long as she didn't disappear completely.

* * *

'Oh, look, Bella...' Lady Dorothy held up a spray of white roses, having successfully squeezed the handles of the secateurs to snip the stem. 'I did it.'

'Well done, you.' Lady Dorothy was beaming at her with such pleasure that Bella had to give her a hug. 'How's your hand feeling?'

'Absolutely fine. Let's get some more. I want to have a lovely big bowl of them on the table for dinner tonight. Freesias, to go with these icebergs because they have such a lovely scent. I do love yellow and white together, don't you? Such a happy combination.'

Excitement had the older woman almost trotting across the garden to where the rose bushes with the bright yellow flowers were. Bella followed her, carrying the flat basket they were using to gather the roses. She *was* thrilled with the fact that Lady Dorothy was able to use the secateurs. The implement took some hand strength and flexibility to operate and even a week ago it would have been too much of an ask. The garden that had always been a passionate interest had been largely ignored since Bella had started working for Lady Dorothy because it had been too frustrating not to be able to do anything more than issue instructions for the gardener.

Yes, Bella was thrilled.

She just wasn't happy.

So much was happening inside her head that, for the last week, her only escape had been to focus on her job and that had been a shining light through the dark turmoil of everything else because she really did love Lady Dorothy. She admired her elegance and applauded her courage and just adored her sense of humour. And the way she was prepared to break convention and have a go at anything—like line dancing, for heaven's sake—was a connection that drew Bella very strongly. In her own way, Oliver Dawson's mother was a bit of a rebel and she understood Bella in a way that Oliver never would.

She took the yellow blooms that were now being cut and laid them in the basket. At any other time, the glorious perfume would have been a delight but right now it was making her feel distinctly queasy.

Bella was getting moments like this with increasing frequency and they certainly weren't confined to the mornings. She could feel how tender her breasts were with every movement of her arms, too. There was no escape from the fact that she was pregnant. And the days were ticking past and Bella still had no idea quite how she was going to handle it.

Watching Lady Dorothy, Bella could see that it was becoming more of a struggle to operate the secateurs. She wasn't giving in to the difficulty, though. Or even the pain. Some people had so much courage and determination.

Like Kate.

Bella was still reeling from the story she'd been told that night when Kate had come back from her serious time with Connor out in the garden. With tears running down her face, she'd told Bella about getting pregnant at fifteen and how she'd known she *ought* to get a termination but she couldn't because she'd already loved that baby.

Part of Bella had been horrified by that. The father of the baby was at best a drop-kick boyfriend. At worst a vicious rapist. Another part of her had understood completely. It was an innocent baby and how could you *not* love it?

The reality of her situation had begun to penetrate then. It was a *baby* that Bella had growing in her own womb. It was no leap at all to feel a protective love for that tiny being. And its father certainly wasn't a drop-kick. As Connor had pointed out, when he'd come in to join the discussion, if she'd gone to a sperm bank and listed the qualities she wanted for a perfect father, Oliver would have been at the top of the list with his good looks and intelligence and impeccable family background.

An abortion had never been an option, had it? No. The curly problem was how to handle the other people involved here. Oliver, of course. And Lady Dorothy. The other grandmother of this baby.

The woman who was finally reaching her physical limit in her current task.

'Do you think that's enough?'

'Absolutely. Look, we've got a whole basket full.'

'Are you good at arranging flowers, Bella?'

Bella sighed. 'The way I arrange flowers is to plonk them in a vase, hold my breath, go wiffle wiffle with the stems and hope for the best.'

Lady Dorothy laughed. 'Wonderful. I can just see my floral art teacher from when I was your age having to reach for her smelling salts. She was such an old fuddy-duddy.' Her hand was trembling quite badly as she laid the secateurs in the basket with the roses. She tucked her arm through Bella's to disguise the evidence of her discomfort. 'Let's go and find a vase.'

With the flowers arranged, albeit haphazardly, Bella

found some anti-inflammatory gel and massaged Lady Dorothy's hands. And then it was time to take her blood-sugar levels and administer her evening dose of insulin. Bella took her blood pressure as well and wrote her daily notes up neatly. Flicking through the notes for the last week brought a wry smile to her lips.

How ironic that she had planned to impress Oliver and make him see what he was missing when she left by doing her job as perfectly as possible. She was performing at her absolute best now but she would never be able to impress the man she loved because, at some point, she had to reveal the fact that she was just as stupid and irresponsible as he'd suspected all along.

She'd asked him to trust her and she'd let him down in the biggest way there was. She'd let her parents and Kate down, too. Most of all, she'd let herself down.

Well…she'd finally learned her lesson.

Bella felt like she'd suddenly become a proper adult in the last week.

She was all grown up.

Maybe she'd known all along that being grown up was a scary and confusing place to be and that was why she'd resisted for so long.

With Lady Dorothy settled comfortably in the conservatory with a glass of sherry, Bella hurried to the kitchen to prepare dinner and think up an excuse for not joining her patient this evening because she knew that Oliver was planning to be there.

She heard the front door open and close as she was setting out Lady Dorothy's special cutlery on the table. She should be getting used to the way her heart skipped a beat and then started racing. The way that knot of longing deep in her belly bloomed and then melted into her veins. It had changed since the revelation of her pregnancy, though. This was more than pure lust. It was more than simply being in love. This was a need for something huge. For the whole world to shift on its axis and create a new *family*. She and Oliver and Lady Dorothy and the baby.

There was no way it could happen. It was so far from being *appropriate* that it was ridiculous. Bella had rehearsed telling Oliver about this pregnancy in her head so many times by now she had every possible scenario covered. At best, she would be made financially secure somewhere else and Oliver would have contact with his child on a strictly negotiated routine. At worst, he would be so disgusted with her irresponsibility he would hate her for ever and order her out of his life and any child care arrangements, financial or other, would be handled by his solicitors.

She couldn't let that happen. Not yet. Not until Lady Dorothy was more independent. At least Bella could be responsible about that. She served the meals onto warmed plates, cutting up one of the pieces of fillet steak so that Lady Dorothy wouldn't need to ask for any assistance. She put the plates in the oven to keep the meals hot and gave the table a final glance, which made her smile. It was just as well the roses were beautiful all by themselves, because the arrangement of them did nothing to enhance them, despite Lady Dorothy's declaration that Bella had hidden, artistic talents. The remnants of that poignant smile were still on her lips as she went to the door of the conservatory.

Oliver had followed a familiar routine. He'd picked

up the mail on his way into the house and helped his mother open the envelopes. There can't have been too much today because now he was helping his mother up from her chair.

'Dinner's in the oven,' Bella told them brightly. 'I've got a few things to do so I'll be in to see you later, Lady Dorothy.'

'Wait…' Lady Dorothy was holding a white card in her hand. She beamed at Bella. 'Did you know about this?'

Bella stopped. There was no help for it now, she had to meet Oliver's gaze as they came closer. And the gaze was intense. As though he wanted something from her. Curiously, he looked worried about her. Was he asking for reassurance?

Bella smiled at him with the intention of pretending that everything was fine. There was nothing to worry about.

She caught her breath when she saw the relief in his dark eyes. When he smiled back at her.

One of *those* smiles. As if she was special and important. Like the one he'd given her when he'd approved of what she was doing for his mother when she'd been an inpatient at St Pat's. When she'd first caught a glimpse of the real Oliver hidden beneath the professional man. When it had touched something so deep inside her she'd known she was in real danger of falling in love with him.

And she'd known they were dangerous waters to even dip her toe into, but what had she done?

Dived in. Completely out of her depth. And now she felt like she was drowning. She had to tell him but…

not yet. Because she couldn't bear the thought of being sent away—physically or emotionally. When she told Oliver about the pregnancy, one thing she could be absolutely sure of was that she'd never see one of those smiles again.

Bella swallowed hard and tried to focus on Lady Dorothy. Her voice came out a little hoarsely. 'What is it?'

'A wedding invitation.' Lady Dorothy sighed happily. 'From your Kate and her Connor. At the beach. Such short notice, though. Only three weeks...'

Bella's smile was ancient history. She felt slightly dizzy. Whose idea had this been? And why hadn't anyone warned her?

'Are you all right, Bella?' Oliver's smile had also vanished. He was looking really worried now. As though it really mattered to him whether she was all right or not. Bella wanted to cry.

'I'm...fine...'

'You did know about this?'

'The wedding?' Bella forced another smile. 'Of course...I'm the bridesmaid.'

'It's so kind of you to get us invited,' Lady Dorothy said. 'I haven't been to a wedding in so long. Oh, my... we've got to think of a gift, Oliver.'

But Oliver knew she hadn't answered the question. He was still staring at Bella.

'It's a small wedding,' she said. 'A few friends and family and colleagues from St Pat's. You're friends with Connor, aren't you?'

'We have a fair bit to do with each other. We often

share spinal surgery cases. And I suppose we get on well. But who wouldn't, with Connor?'

Oliver was looking vaguely surprised, as if the notion of being friends with someone was alien. Bella felt the same kind of sadness for him she had when she'd learned that he'd had an unhappy childhood. Did he even realise how much he was missing out on in life? She wanted to reach out and take hold of his hand. Let him know that she could sense things about him that only someone who loved him would be able to sense. And that she cared enough to make it better.

How amazing that she could have got to a point where she thought she was the thing that was missing from the life of a man who had once intimidated her to the extent that she'd felt she wasn't good enough at anything. She would be good for him but he wasn't in a space where he could recognise it. She hadn't had enough time to impress him. And as soon as he knew that she'd lied to him about being safe to have sex with, any chance at all to impress Oliver Dawson would be obliterated. Oh, help. She had to get out of here before she disgraced herself and burst into tears.

'And Lady Dorothy's been invited because she's an important person in my life right now.' Bella ducked closer to give Lady Dorothy a kiss on her cheek. 'Now, go and have your dinner before it gets cold and before your blood sugar takes a dive. I'll see you soon.'

And with that, Bella escaped. Straight to her room where she grabbed her mobile phone and pushed the first rapid dial entry.

'My God, Kate,' she said, as soon as the call was

answered. 'What *are* you up to? You've invited the *Dawsons* to the wedding?'

'It was Connor's idea. And he's right. They're going to be a part of our family in some way now.'

'They don't know that.'

She could hear Kate sigh. 'You have to tell him some time, Bella.'

'I know…but…I'm not ready.'

'The longer you leave it, the harder it's going to be, hon.'

'I know, but…' Bella could feel tears threatening.

'But what?' Kate asked gently.

'The longer I leave it, the safer it'll be.'

'What do you mean?'

But Bella couldn't articulate the fear. The idea that Oliver would be so angry or that Lady Dorothy would be so appalled at the scandal in the family that they could somehow persuade her that a termination was the only way to manage this disaster. Facing Lady Dorothy's disappointment and severing the bond she had with the older woman was almost as daunting a prospect as facing Oliver's wrath and Bella wasn't entirely sure she was strong enough to stand up to them. So she wanted to wait until she was past the point where it might be viewed as nothing more than a simple medical procedure. Until it became indisputably a baby for everyone involved and not just an accidental pregnancy.

'Things can happen,' she offered. 'Especially in the first trimester. I…might lose it.' The tears couldn't be held back now. Maybe that would solve all sorts of problems but she *really* didn't want to lose this baby. Oliver's baby. Kate heard her strangled sob.

'That's highly unlikely, Bells. Look, I've got my sixteen-week scan coming up next week. Come with me and we'll get a check-up for you, too.'

'I can't do that. Not at St Pat's, anyway. What if Oliver found out?'

There was a silence. They both knew that it was only a question of time before Oliver was going to find out.

'Nobody needs to know about the scan,' Kate said quietly. 'But you need to know that everything's OK. And you need to start taking care of yourself.' She chuckled. 'I'll set Connor onto you if you don't behave. He's become the world's expert on how mothers-to-be need to look after themselves.'

Mothers-to-be.

She was going to be a *mother*.

So was Kate.

Bella's voice wobbled. 'Connor's really happy about it, isn't he?'

'He's over the moon. I still can't believe it. It's… I'm so happy, Bella.'

'I know. It's wonderful.'

'I thought this pregnancy would be the last thing he wanted and that it would be the thing that broke us up but it's brought us closer together. I had no idea you could be so much in love with someone and not understand something so huge.'

'Mmm.' Bella knew you could be so much in love with someone and not know them very well at all. How did that happen? How could she be so sure that she could love Oliver for the rest of his life if he gave her the chance but the only really personal thing she knew about him was that he liked fast food?

'You could be wrong about Oliver, you know,' Kate was saying now. 'He might surprise you. He might like you a lot more than you think he does.'

Bella shook her head, her breath escaping in a quiet groan. Didn't Kate understand that she was encouraging a fantasy? Making the bubble bigger? The bubble that Bella was so scared of having to pop?

'He liked you enough to get you pregnant.'

'He thinks I'm an idiot.'

'He doesn't know you, then. That's why Connor thought the wedding invitation was a good idea. It will give us all a chance to get to know each other a little better.'

'Why did you bring the date forward so much?'

Kate laughed. 'So I'll still fit my dress. It was either that or wait until after the baby and…well, neither of us wanted to wait.'

Of course they didn't. They loved each other and they were excited about becoming parents.

Parents.

'Oh, God,' Bella groaned. 'Mum and Dad will be there, won't they?'

'Of course. I was talking to them yesterday. They're wondering why they haven't heard from you this week.' There was gentle admonition in Kate's voice. 'They'll understand, you know. They'll support you, just as much as Connor and I will.'

The support from Kate and Connor was already a safety net that Bella felt she didn't deserve. She could live with them if she wanted. For as long as she wanted. They could find a bigger house that could accommodate an extended family and the babies could grow up being almost twins. Bella could mother them both when Kate was ready to go back to work. And, yes, she knew that her parents wouldn't abandon her but they would, inevitably, be shocked.

'They'll be so disappointed that I'm going to be a single mother.' Another sob escaped and Bella had to sniff loudly. 'And then they'll be at the wedding and so will Oliver and… Oh, Kate, how *could* you? I'm not ready for any of this.'

'I'm sorry, love.' Kate sounded contrite. 'I guess we didn't think things through enough. You can tell your mum and dad without telling them who the father is and that way they can't say anything by accident. And maybe Oliver won't want to come.'

Lady Dorothy would, though.

Unless…

Unless *she* dropped the bombshell first. Oliver definitely wouldn't attend then and she'd be fired from her job and the timing might work quite well because she was planning to cat-sit for Kate and Connor while they went on their honeymoon and…

And her head was spinning like a top and the wave of nausea was the strongest yet.

'I have to go.' The statement was urgent. 'I think I'm going to be sick.'

CHAPTER TEN

THE bombshell was impossible to drop.

Lady Dorothy was so excited about attending the wedding that she demanded a more vigorous exercise routine and put her heart and soul into gaining strength and balance so that she could cope with walking on sand.

'I won't take my stick,' she declared. 'Oliver will be there if I need any support but I want to get dressed up and not look like an invalid.' Her eyes had held an appeal Bella had no chance of resisting. 'I want to look like *me* again.'

How could she have taken that away from the old lady she was so fond of? The outing would be a reward for all the hard work she'd put in over so many weeks since she'd become ill. She wanted to show her son that she could be independent again and rejoin society. Maybe she wanted to show that she wasn't going to be a burden for him in the years to come. It didn't matter what she was trying to prove, however. What mattered was that it was so important to her and that she started every day glowing with determination and pride in what she was achieving.

The achievements spiralled upwards as the days went

by. Life inevitably became busier for Bella and she was slipping away from the Dawson household at increasingly frequent intervals to help Kate and Connor with all the wedding arrangements. That prompted Lady Dorothy to increase her independence even further. She learned to manage testing her blood sugar by herself again and could—almost—manage her insulin injections. She had also agreed to wear a personal alarm around her neck on the occasions that both Bella and Oliver were absent and that way she could call for help if she felt a hypoglycaemic episode coming on or if she lost her balance and fell over.

The changes were a double-edged sword. Not ruining Lady Dorothy's excited anticipation had the added benefit of letting the Dawsons know that they would be able to cope without Bella in their lives. It would, at least, remove any guilt in having to abandon her private patient if she got fired from her position.

Knowing that she was becoming dispensable didn't make the prospect of dropping the bombshell any easier, though. If Bella was really honest with herself, the biggest reason she couldn't do it was the change she was watching in Oliver.

Ever since the day the wedding invitation had arrived and she'd seen that look of concern in his intense gaze... Ever since he'd smiled at her again in that way that made her feel so special, something was happening between them.

He was spending more time in her company. Drawing her into conversations she couldn't resist, like when he'd talked her through the surgery that Wally had had and brought her up to date with the wonderful progress her old patient was making.

'He's missing his line-dancing classes,' Oliver told her, and there was a gleam of genuine amusement in his eyes. 'Might be time for me to have another one myself.'

Bella had been gobsmacked. She made some joke about how embarrassing it would be for Oliver if it got around St Pat's that he was taking line-dancing lessons and nothing more had been said but it was becoming more and more obvious that Oliver was reaching out. Trying to close the gap between them. Actually trying to make her *laugh*?

Like the day he'd told her she didn't need to prepare dinner on the housekeeper's day off. *He* would cook, he'd said, and then he'd arrived home laden with paper sacks from the fast-food restaurant.

'It's an old family tradition,' Lady Dorothy explained. 'Disgusting but delicious. Our little secret.'

If only he knew how much harder he was making everything.

Because it was irresistible. She was being drawn into this family. Made to feel as if she could be an accepted part of it and Oliver was showing her, all over again, the reasons she had fallen in love with him.

The very real love he had for his mother.

The streak of humour that lay mostly hidden beneath such a controlled exterior.

That hint that he would actually revel in the chance to rebel if he thought he could get away with it.

He got that from his mother. He had her strength of character and single-minded determination as well. He just hadn't learned to balance things. Had he learned as a child that friendship and fun had to be sacrificed in order to retain control of what was happening in his life? Bella knew she could teach him otherwise if she had enough time.

She didn't have the luxury of time so was it so dreadful to put off the confession that would spell an end to what was beginning to happen? She would never have it again. Maybe it was knowing that this was the very last time in her life that she could embrace fantasy before stepping into the responsibilities of being completely grown up. Being a *mother* and not a carefree young woman with the possibilities of anything she could dream of ahead of her in life.

Was it so terrible to want one more night with Oliver? Because that seemed to be where this new attitude was heading.

Things were improving.

Glimpses of the old Bella were returning. It had taken some effort but it had been well worth it. He'd seen a gleam of…admiration, perhaps when he'd gone as far as suggesting that she give him another line-dancing lesson.

He would have done it, too, but she'd been evasive.

He'd made her laugh, though, offering to cook and then turning up with hamburgers and French fries.

She seemed happy to talk to him too and it was so easy to talk about things that always bored the kind of women he'd always dated. Medical stuff, which was all he really had to talk about, wasn't it? Had he really dismissed Bella as a somewhat ditzy young nurse? She was smart and things she probably hadn't learned in her training had been absorbed on the job. She actually seemed fascinated by the intricacies of neurosurgery and the questions she asked were intelligent.

What stayed with Oliver during his days at work was the way she could centre on the people involved, not just the medical details. Bella cared about patients she hadn't even met and he would find himself following them up in more detail, even asking about things in his patients' lives that had nothing to do with the case, just so he could make them more real for Bella and hold her interest even more keenly. The odd thing was, he was getting more interested himself. Connecting with his patients in a way he never had before.

Bella Graham really was the most intriguing woman he'd ever met.

And she was...gorgeous.

The idea that having a relationship with her would undermine his controlled life to a dangerous degree was fraying around the edges now. With every passing day, Oliver was craving more than just trying to make the old Bella reappear from that unusually restrained version.

He was craving *her*.

He wanted Bella. No, he *needed* her.

His control finally broke one evening the following week, when there was a particularly spectacular sunset happening.

'Come with me,' he said. 'I want to show you something.'

He led her down through the garden.

'I've never been this far,' Bella said. 'I keep meaning to find the steps and go and have a swim at the beach. Is it safe?'

'The beach? Yes, it's perfectly safe.' Going this far with him, the way he was feeling right now? Probably not.

'It's good swimming.' Oliver had to clear his throat. 'You need to stay on the steps going down, though. The cliff can be a bit crumbly in places. Here, this is what I wanted to show you.'

The old summer house was at its best on an evening like this, warmed by the glow of the sunset and with a clear view of the ocean and the changing light.

'It's my personal haven,' Oliver told Bella. 'The place I always feel most at peace with the world.'

Would she understand how significant it was to bring her here?

She seemed to. She was standing so close to him and when she looked up, Oliver was sure he was going to drown in what he could see in her eyes.

An almost childlike mix of appreciation and wonder and excitement. But there was nothing childlike about the way her pupils dilated and her lips parted. It was pure woman and utterly irresistible.

The first time they'd kissed Oliver wasn't quite sure how it had happened. One moment they'd been standing there and the next they'd been all over each other. But this time he savoured every microsecond, dipping his head with infinite slowness to bring their lips into contact. Maybe he was giving Bella the chance to pull away if she didn't want this. More likely, he was finding the exquisite torture of delayed gratification too alluring. And Bella didn't pull away. She didn't close her eyes either. She was watching him and it was like looking into an emotional mirror. He could swear she wanted this just as much as he did.

The built-in seating was more than wide enough to serve as a bed and, if the cushions were past their use-by date, neither of them noticed or cared. Like the kiss, Oliver slowed things down as far as he was physically capable of doing. He undressed Bella, touching her skin as though it was the first time. In a way, it was. They had been so inflamed by passion last time, he'd barely noticed detail. He was noticing now. How smooth her skin was. How delicious it tasted. How just one touch of his tongue could make her nipples tighten into the most amazingly hard buttons that begged to be softened by enough extra attention.

And the way Bella responded to his touch was like nothing Oliver had ever experienced. If his first encounter with her had been the most mind-blowingly exciting sex he'd ever had, this was the most tender. Did Bella feel it touching something so deep in her soul that he couldn't even recognise what it was?

Maybe she did.

Maybe that was why he saw those tears in her eyes when he held her gently as they finally returned to reality.

Not that he got a chance to talk to her about it.

'It's almost dark,' Bella murmured. 'It must be getting late.' She pulled away from him. '*I'm* getting late. I'm supposed to be at Kate's by now. There's so much to do with only a few days till the wedding.'

She was still moving as she spoke, getting off the wide seat and leaving a space that felt unbearable empty beside him. She was getting dressed at the speed of light despite having to search for items in the dimness of a dying day.

And then she was gone and Oliver groaned softly. He probably wouldn't see her for days now with the chaos of the last-minute wedding preparations.

He wanted to see her again.

Soon.

CHAPTER ELEVEN

IT WAS a perfect day for a beach wedding.

The perfect beach to be having it on.

In the glow of a setting sun, the huge rock forma-
tion that looked like a crouching lion was a dramatic
backdrop to the long stretch of sand left glistening by
the retreating tide. Other people using the beach were
keeping a respectful distance and the waves were far
enough away for the occasional surfer to be nothing
more than a part of this wonderful setting.

The small crowd of guests were standing in a semi-
circular group, leaving a sandy track that had been
strewn with rose petals for the bride and her bridesmaid
to walk though. One guest was not standing, however.
A fold-out chair had been positioned at the front, on the
edge of the circle, to give Lady Dorothy Dawson a clear
view of the proceedings. She was wearing a silk dress
with a matching jacket and hat in shades of gold that
would not have looked out of place in a gathering of the
Royal family. Bella had been there when she'd tried on
the outfit and chosen her accessories last week. The garnet necklace she wore was perfect for her outfit. It was
just a shame that she couldn't wear the matching ring
because the joints of her fingers were still misshapen.

Beside her, of course, stood her son, wearing the dinner suit Bella had seen once before that made him look so impossible gorgeous. So unattainable.

That unattainability had been an illusion, though, hadn't it? If things were only different now—if she hadn't been so irresponsibly stupid, she might have had a chance of having a perfect ending to the love story she was currently living. Oliver might have been unable to help himself falling in love with her and he would have swept her up into his arms and carried her off into the sunset of a blissful future.

But this was real life and there was an emotional storm coming. Painful accusations and probably lots of tears. Quite possibly, there was going to be hostility that she would have to deal with for the rest of her life—on a regular basis—if Oliver insisted on having a part in his child's life.

It was both frightening and heartbreaking.

But Bella couldn't afford to think about that right now. Not on Kate's special day. By tacit agreement, the subject hadn't been mentioned so far today. This ceremony was about a romance that had led to a happy ending and it marked the beginning of the future she would have chosen for her favourite person on earth.

Instead, as Bella let her senses soak in Oliver's presence, she remembered that perfect time with him in the summer house. A memory that she could hold close to her heart for a lifetime. Such bitter-sweet, heartbreakingly tender lovemaking, knowing that it was the last time. Knowing that she could be perfectly truthful in telling him that a condom wasn't necessary. She could never have had that time if he'd known that she was pregnant.

And Lady Dorothy wouldn't be here, beaming with happiness, either.

She'd been right not to drop the bombshell but the timer was ticking so loudly now Bella was afraid it was going to spoil her pleasure in this wonderful celebration. She just had to make sure it didn't spoil anyone else's pleasure.

She walked slowly down the sand aisle behind her beloved aunt.

Kate was wearing a simple, ivory dress that suited her perfectly. Slim fitting to her hips from where it fell in feminine swirls, it had a low, cowl neckline and no sleeves. Her hair was only partly confined by a pretty twist that took hair away from her face and into an intricate knot at the back of her head. The rest fell in a glorious, dark ripple down her back but was held in place enough by the twist to cope with any sea breeze. Tiny white flowers woven into the twisted section stood out against the dark gleam of her hair like jewels.

The dress was fitted enough to show the slight swell of Kate's belly. Bella's dress was just as clingy but it would be weeks before she started to show and she loved this dress, which was the colour of the sea on a sunny day. Kate had said it was a perfect match for both Bella's eyes and the beach setting.

Lady Dorothy and Oliver had sworn they could cope so Bella had stayed with Kate last night so that they could spend the day together to prepare for this important event. There had been appointments at the nail salon and hairdresser and it had been like she had been getting ready for her own wedding.

As they reached the end of the petal-strewn aisle and Kate moved to stand beside Connor in front of the celebrant, Bella could feel Oliver's stare like a touch on her skin. Her head turned of its own accord.

Had she known that he would think she looked beautiful? Desirable? She couldn't deny that she'd hoped he would and his expression now was exactly what she'd dreamed it might be.

The colour that Bella could feel warming her cheeks was more than pleasure. Or even mirrored desire. Part of it was a touch of guilt because she knew perfectly well that it hadn't been purely for Lady Dorothy's benefit or even for the chance of one more night with Oliver that she'd delayed the inevitable confession.

She'd wanted *this*.

She'd wanted Oliver to see her looking this good. Dressed for a wedding. To see him dressed in that suit again.

She'd wanted the fantasy of being able to close her eyes for a moment during the wedding vows and imagine what it would be like if the words were being spoken by herself. And Oliver.

The vows were simple. Heartfelt declarations of love and the promises to nurture that love for as long as they both lived. The guests were close enough to hear every word and to see the tender kiss exchanged as the vows ended. And nobody missed the way Kate took her hands, still enclosed by both of Connor's, to rest against her belly before they finally broke their first kiss as man and wife.

The wedding celebrant, a middle-aged woman called Sarah, smiled mistily.

'Connor and Kate are celebrating their love for each other in more ways than getting married today,' she told the guests. 'They'd like to share with you all the joy they have in expecting their first baby. They've become more than simply man and wife in this lovely ceremony. They've become a *family*.'

A surprised, delighted murmur came from the guests. Bella was close enough to hear Lady Dorothy's excited whisper.

'Oh... Oliver, isn't that wonderful? A darling baby. How *perfect*.'

Kate and Connor were smiling at each other in a way that shut out anybody else on the planet. Sarah was raising her voice to be heard over the murmurs.

'Please enjoy this time on Piha beach while some photographs are being taken. Kate and Connor will be joining you in the marquee for the picnic supper very soon.'

The group began to move now, dispersing in different directions. Some went to find people they knew to talk to. Others started making their way to the marquee set up by the spit-roast company that was catering the low-key wedding breakfast. Other people were staying to watch the photographer, who was ushering Kate and Bella into position for the first shots.

'Just a couple,' he said. 'I want to get the bride and groom near the waves while the light's this good. We'll do any family shots later.'

From the corner of her eye Bella could see her parents being dragged towards the food. Her younger brothers and sisters were pretty much grown up now but one of her brothers was a poor medical student and the baby of the family was only nineteen and still a bottomless pit when it came to food. She watched them laughing and jostling each other and felt like she was standing on another planet. Her siblings still had no idea she had ruined her plans for her exciting overseas adventures, not to mention getting married to a man she loved, who loved her and settling down to the business of creating her own family.

With Kate's agreement, Bella had put off telling her parents when they'd arrived yesterday as well. They both knew that the support would be there when Bella needed it but it would be a shock that needed absorbing and if Bella told them now, it would totally overshadow any joy they had in being a part of Kate's wedding. And even though they had no idea that the father of her baby was present at the wedding, the Dawsons were bound to pick up the impression that something was going on. Having all the most important people in her life in one place like this was incredibly stressful. Bella would have loved to have been heading for a glass or two of champagne herself but she couldn't and only two other people there knew why. What if somebody offered her a glass and guessed why she was refusing it?

She could almost hear one of her twin sisters laughing and saying, *'Good heavens, Bella, that's not like you. You're not pregnant or something, are you?'*

And what if Oliver happened to be standing nearby?

Oh…*help*. How on earth was she going to get through the next few hours?

The photographer was now leading Kate and Connor

away for their photographs and Bella found herself standing alone. She could see Oliver preparing to help his mother get up from the low chair. How long were they planning to stay? Long enough for her to have to introduce them to her parents? Her mother had said she was keen to meet Bella's intriguing new employer.

Bella could feel the tension escalating rapidly as she saw that Oliver was starting to walk towards her. Lady Dorothy was still sitting in the chair, staring towards the sea, apparently watching the bride and groom have their photographs taken.

Turning her head away with something like panic bubbling within, Bella saw that the happy couple were walking hand in hand, close to the waves. Their heads were bent so close together they seemed to be touching and the photographer was behind them, capturing the tender moment that had the dramatic backdrop of Lion Rock.

A very real moment.

And here she was, living a lie. She'd been so determined to stay inside that fantasy bubble for as long as she could and Kate had been right. The longer she was leaving it, the harder it was getting. She'd made it so much worse by allowing herself that extra time with Oliver. Lying to him yet again, albeit by omission. The kind of lie that had always seemed to be far less of a sin. Until now.

Bella hated herself right then. She deserved whatever was coming and it was coming soon, she could tell. Good grief, she felt like she might explode at any moment.

And Oliver was simply smiling at her.

'You look gorgeous,' he said.

'Thank you.' Her throat was so tight it was hard to get any words out.

'You're about to lose this, though.' He reached out and his hand touched her hair. Bella had a hairstyle that matched Kate's, with a twisted section to hold the loose length in place. Tiny, blue flowers and been wound into her hair to match her dress but one of them must have worked loose. And Oliver was fixing it?

Oh…*God*…

Bella could feel the touch of his hand. She could feel the warmth of it and it was all she could do not to tilt her face so that it was cupped by his palm. And he was leaning closer so that he could see what he was doing. So close that Bella could feel his breath on her face. She could feel the intensity of his gaze even before she raised her eyes to meet it.

'You're beautiful, Bella,' Oliver said softly. 'I want to kiss you.'

Bella's mouth went as dry as the sand further up the beach. 'No, you don't.' Desperation made her words come out with a faint hiss.

Oliver's eyes widened as if she'd slapped him but he didn't move away. If anything, he dipped his head slightly. His mouth was close enough…close enough to kiss, heaven help her.

'Your m-mother's here,' she stammered. 'And half the consultants from St Pat's. It's not…not appropriate, remember?'

'I don't think I care,' Oliver murmured. 'I still want to kiss you.'

Good grief…this wasn't a part of any fantasy Bella

had been able to conjure up about them both being dressed up and at a wedding. It could have been, except that it was far too much to have hoped for, even when she was trying to make herself irresistibly attractive.

She couldn't let it happen. How embarrassed would Oliver be if he made his interest in her public—in front of so many of his colleagues? Things were hard enough now. Too hard, in fact. Bella couldn't live with the lie any longer.

'*I'm* inappropriate,' she said with increasing desperation. 'Irresponsible.'

'Not from where I'm standing,' Oliver said. 'In fact, I don't think I've ever seen anyone being quite so responsible about their job as I've seen you being in the last few weeks. My mother thinks you're an angel. She adores you.'

'She doesn't know how irresponsible I am.' Bella could actually feel the blood draining from a part of her brain. Leaving it very empty and clear. She knew what she had to do. 'I lied to you, Oliver.'

'Sorry?' He did step back now and the look he was giving her was bewildered. 'What on earth are you talking about, Bella?'

'I lied to you about being on the Pill.'

She could see the way Oliver became very still.

'Well, I didn't *lie* exactly…but I didn't correct you when you made the wrong assumption and I should have.'

Bella knew she was babbling but the way he seemed to draw into himself until he was standing there like a stone statue was so horrible. The warmth had gone from his eyes completely. No admiration or desire there now. The look Bella was getting was cold. Fierce, almost.

'What are you trying to tell me, Bella?'

It was now or never. Her voice came out as a strangled kind of whisper.

'I'm pregnant, Oliver.'

He still looked fierce but she could see that the news hadn't sunk in. He didn't understand the implication.

'Oliver, it's *your* baby I'm pregnant with.'

'Oh, *my*...' The soft cry came from just behind Oliver and it made them both turn. How on earth had Lady Dorothy managed to get out of that chair all by herself?

It must have been difficult. Time consuming. But somehow she had managed it. And she had timed it so that she couldn't help but hearing the fateful words despite how softly Bella had spoken.

Oh, God, what had she done? Just gone ahead without thinking of the repercussions and this was going to ruin Kate's special day. Bella felt a wave of nausea so powerful she had to press her hand against her mouth.

'Oh...' Lady Dorothy's gasp was deeply concerned. 'You're so pale, dear. I think you'd better sit down.'

'I'm sorry,' Bella managed. 'I didn't mean you to hear that. I didn't want—'

'This is neither the time nor the place,' Oliver cut in. He looked as pale as Bella clearly was. 'Go and sit down, Bella. Would you like me to get you a glass of water?'

'N-no, thank you.'

A wave of misery washed over Bella at Oliver's tone. The kind of tone she had heard many times before. When she was an unimportant junior cog in the wheel of his operating theatre. She knew he had to be in shock but this was exactly like speaking to that intimidating neurosurgeon, not the man she'd come to know. And love. This was Oliver in professional mode. Taking control of a situation that was both unexpected and potentially calamitous. The man who had looked, such a short time ago, as though he wanted nothing more than to kiss her senseless seemed like a figment of her imagination.

'I'm going to take my mother home,' Oliver continued in that calm, expressionless voice. 'When you're finished here, I suggest you come and join us. Obviously, we need to talk.' He had his hand under his mother's elbow, turning her, but Lady Dorothy was looking torn. She bit her lip, turning her worried gaze from Bella to Oliver. And then she looked around her, at the milling guests and the bride and groom who were now walking back towards the gathering.

'We're not going to make a scene and spoil Kate and Connor's wedding, Oliver,' she said decisively. 'In fact, I'd like a glass of champagne, please. And I think a glass of water for Bella is a very good idea.'

Oliver was looking stunned that he was being outbid for control of the situation.

'This is a very special occasion,' Lady Dorothy continued. 'Not only because it's such a lovely wedding but it's the first time I've been dressed up to go out for months. The first time I've been to a beach for *years*.'

Lady Dorothy was smiling at Bella now and the message was clear. A kind of 'keep calm and carry on' message. She looked as though everything in her world was absolutely fine and she certainly hadn't overheard any shattering news. She also looked as though she'd done this before. As if she was employing a well-practised skill. She patted Bella arm.

'Help me back to my chair, dear, while Oliver goes and gets those drinks for us.'

The photographer was rounding up all the members of the Graham family now. Bella would need to join them for a group photograph soon.

Walking slowly and assisting Lady Dorothy, Bella watched Oliver's back as he stalked towards the marquee. She sighed.

'He's very angry,' she said quietly. 'And I can't blame him.'

'He's shaken up, that's all,' Lady Dorothy said calmly. 'He needs a bit of time to get used to the idea.'

The look she gave Bella was, amazingly, almost mischievous. It made Bella remember the things Lady Dorothy had said when she'd been trying to persuade Bella to take the position as her private nurse. The startling admission that her son was a bit 'stuffy'. That it would do him good to be 'shaken up a little'.

Surely she wasn't relegating the fact that Bella was pregnant into the 'shaking someone up a little' category? This was more than a little shake. It was a 'turn the world upside down and rattle it as hard as you can' kind of movement. But Lady Dorothy settled calmly into the chair, nodding her head as though affirming her words.

'Running away is never a good way to deal with anything.'

Bella's eyes were still widening as she regarded this extraordinary woman who was old enough to be her grandmother. 'I thought you'd be angry, too.'

'Angry? Good heavens, no. Surprised, yes, but I know what's been going on, dear.'

Bella could feel herself blushing. 'But—'

Lady Dorothy made a tutting sound. 'I may be old but I'm not senile, Bella. Or blind. Anyone could see the way you two have been watching each other. Heavens above…that day I was out in the garden, Oliver couldn't take his eyes off you when you were walking back into the house. And you had to have one more peek before you disappeared.'

Bella couldn't deny it. She had felt that stare. And she'd seen him turning to his mother when she couldn't resist looking back. What she hadn't seen was that Lady Dorothy had been watching her.

'I was hoping something might happen between you,' Lady Dorothy continued. 'But I wasn't expecting this, I have to admit.' The look she gave Bella was serious. 'My son isn't a man to shirk his responsibilities. He'll do the right thing.'

'Bella?' Kate was calling her. 'We need you for the family photos.'

With a nod, Bella went to join the group. The 'right thing'.

What was that?

Did Lady Dorothy mean that he would offer to marry her?

Because it was the 'right thing' to do or because he wanted to?

She'd never know, would she?

Oliver handed his mother the glass of champagne but Bella wasn't there to accept the water. She was in the group of people that clustered around the bride and groom. Quite a large group.

Lady Dorothy took a sip of her champagne. She was watching the group being arranged as well.

'What a lovely family,' was all she said.

Oliver tried to close his eyes but they wouldn't cooperate. Neither would they focus on any member of the Graham family that wasn't Bella. She still looked a little pale perhaps, but not enough to attract attention. And she was smiling. He saw the way her mother touched her cheek and how her younger sisters, who looked to be in their early twenties and were obviously twins, were jostling for the prime position of being next to Bella.

Twins in the family. Good grief...

I can't *marry* her, he thought desperately.

'Why ever not?'

Oh, God, the words must have escaped.

'She...' What was that word Bella kept throwing back at him? 'She's... It's not appropriate.'

Lady Dorothy made a snorting sound. 'That's a ridiculous thing to say, Oliver. It will be a lucky man indeed that gets chosen by Bella. She's adorable.' Her mouth twitched. 'It's pretty obvious that you *like* her. At least I hope it is.'

Oliver was silent. Partly because it was excruciatingly embarrassing to have his mother comment on his sex life at all, let alone suggest that he would be taking a woman he had no feelings for at all to bed. And he couldn't deny that he liked Bella, although *like* was far too insipid a word for any feelings that Bella Graham stirred in him. It would have to do for the moment. He certainly couldn't think of another one while he was still feeling so shocked by this...betrayal?

'She's...' Again, Oliver was lost for a word. How did you sum up someone with Bella's exuberance? Her confident, bubbly, devil-may-care, let's-break-the-rules approach to life? One that inevitably led to disaster? 'She's *flighty*.'

Worse, she was untrustworthy.

She'd lied to him. OK, it was his fault as well. He'd been just as irresponsible, hadn't he? And maybe that was what was making him feel so angry. He'd wanted to be just like Bella and embrace the freedom of ignoring consequences. And he'd known it was a stupid thing to do. The one time he'd decided to take a leaf out of someone like Bella's book and not step away from such overwhelming temptation, and look where it had led. People were going to get hurt by the repercussions.

'She's a joy,' his mother corrected him.

Oliver did manage to close his eyes for a moment now. Yes...that was a much better word. Joy implied happiness. Light. The kind of brightness that Bella left in a room even after she'd gone somewhere else. With a sigh, he opened his eyes and looked at her family again and this time, he was aware of an odd, unsettling, yearning sensation. That feeling of missing out again, without being able to articulate precisely what it was he was missing out on.

Except that this time it was easy. It was the close bonds evident in this group of people. The picture of a family.

'She wants something out of life that I could never give her,' he said.

'Like what?'

'Overseas travel. *Fun*. A dozen kids.' And a man who could keep up with her and embrace a life of chaos. A lucky man, his mother had said. And she'd be right.

A man who would end up raising Oliver's child?

Now, *that* was a very disturbing thought.

His mother was silent for a long moment. Then she asked quietly, 'What is it that *you* want, Oliver?'

To get off this emotional merry-go-round, he thought vehemently. It was too much. It was confusing. He needed something solid to cling to and wasn't that a lesson he'd learned long ago? That feelings that hurt could be controlled if you could push them far enough away. Bury them with the things that you *could* control. Things that might not bring happiness but would, at least, bring satisfaction.

'To do my job to the best of my ability,' he said aloud. His words echoed in his own ears, sounding like he was reading from a manifest or job description or something. It wasn't enough, was it? He searched for something he could add to satisfy himself as much as his mother.

'To do the right thing,' he heard himself say. Maybe he could add that he wanted to be successful. To know that he'd contributed in a positive way to the lives of people around him and not caused any harm. Oliver cleared his throat to add his final thought.

'To carry on the kind of contribution to society that you've always done through your charity work.' Good grief, now he sounded positively pompous. Stuffy. Exactly like the impression everybody had of him anyway?

'Is that all?'

Oliver blinked. 'Isn't it enough?'

'No.' Lady Dorothy drank the last of her champagne and looked up at her son. 'You're being given the chance to have something that I was never able to give you, no matter how much I wanted to.'

'Which is?'

'A family,' Lady Dorothy said softly. 'A *real* family.'

Oliver could hear the undertone of sadness in her voice and it added a different kind of hurt to the emotional ride still trying to whirl him around. He'd tried, for as long as he could remember, to make his mother happy. To make her proud of him. To make up for the empty place his father had left in their lives and their hearts. He hadn't succeeded, had he?

'You know what it's like to have a father who didn't care enough,' Lady Dorothy said, even more quietly. 'Is that a legacy you'd want to pass on to your own child?'

That sadness was palpable now and part of it was his own. Of course he didn't want to pass it on. Maybe the determination that he never would was why he'd never found someone he would consider marrying. How long would he have kept up the half-hearted search? Long enough for the choice to be taken away? It wasn't beyond the realms of possibility that he could have found himself alone and childless in years to come because he'd put off taking a risk, knowing what the repercussions might be from making the wrong choice.

'I think we could probably leave soon, without it being seen as impolite,' Lady Dorothy said. 'I'm suddenly feeling rather tired. And you're right. This is neither the time nor the place for you and Bella to be talking. There'll be plenty of time for that.'

* * *

The photographer had finished with the more formal pictures now. He was ready to capture the social part of the occasion and the closest guests were the old lady in the chair and the man standing beside her, looking far too sombre.

'Let's have a smile,' he suggested. 'This is a wedding after all.'

CHAPTER TWELVE

WHO ever said that tomorrow never came?

It was here now and it was the hardest thing Bella had ever done, returning to the Dawsons' house.

'We'll talk tomorrow' had been Oliver's parting words when he'd taken his mother home from the wedding.

Kate and Connor had left this morning, for their tropical island honeymoon in Rarotonga. Her family had gone home as well, with Bella assuring them that she was fine. She would have to tell them the truth very soon but not just yet. Not until had spoken properly to the father of this baby she was carrying.

But she felt very alone now.

And very scared.

She let herself into the Dawson mansion by a side door near the kitchen that she had a key for. The kitchen was empty and, being a Sunday, the housekeeper was having her day off. It was supposed to be Bella's day off as well, because it was the day of the week that Oliver was most likely to be at home and available if his mother needed assistance but, as often as not, in the last weeks he would be called in for some emergency and Bella hadn't minded. She was being paid quite well enough to be expected to be here twenty-four seven.

She knew where she'd probably find her employer. On a quiet Sunday morning, Lady Dorothy loved to sit in a corner of the conservatory and listen to a radio programme that featured hymns.

'I've always loved getting dressed up and going to church,' she'd told Bella. 'Not that I've done it nearly often enough in recent years.'

Maybe she'd decided to do it today after the pleasure in dressing up to go to Kate's wedding yesterday. If she had, then Oliver would have accompanied her.

But Lady Dorothy was in her usual spot amongst the potted palm trees. Her face lit up in a smile as she saw Bella approaching. The smile widened when her gaze dropped and she saw what Bella was carrying.

'Oh…you've brought Bib. I'm so pleased.'

'Are you sure about this?' Bella crouched beside the plastic carry cage. 'She's not really a kitten any more and she can be quite demanding if she doesn't get the attention she wants.'

'Can't we all?' Lady Dorothy murmured. 'All the more reason to bring her here while Kate and Connor are away on their honeymoon. She might have got lonely with you only popping over a couple of times a day. How awful would it have been if she'd run away?'

'That's true.' Bella opened the door and Bib ventured out without hesitation. With a flick of a fluffy, grey tail, she sniffed the air and started to investigate her new surroundings. Within seconds she was sharpening her claws on the trunk of the nearest palm tree.

'Bad cat,' Bella admonished, picking her up. Bib

started purring loudly but then wriggled to get down. She trotted to Lady Dorothy's chair, leapt up into her lap and then settled into a fluffy ball, still purring.

Lady Dorothy stroked the cat. And smiled.

Bella tried to smile back but her lips wobbled. 'W-where's Oliver?' she asked quietly. 'I think it's time I talked to him.'

'Of course. I'm not sure he's up yet.'

'He hasn't been up to see you?' Bella glanced at her watch, horrified. It was nearly ten a.m.

'Don't worry.' A quiet pride wrapped itself around Lady Dorothy's words. 'I tested my blood sugar myself. And I could have called Oliver to help me with my insulin injection but I didn't need to.'

'Oh…that's wonderful. Well done, you.'

'Oliver might be having a swim. Or using one of those dreadful fitness machines he's so fond of. Do you want to go downstairs and find him?'

Bella shook her head sharply. No way was she going to go downstairs. The last thing Oliver would appreciate would be having conversation they had to have if he was dripping wet and probably half-naked.

She drew in a deep breath and clamped her lips together to stop them trembling but it was impossible to hold back the sting of tears. She blinked hard and willed them away, dipping her head and pretending to fuss with the catch on the carry-cage.

'You care rather a lot about Oliver, don't you, love?' It was an observation rather than a question.

Bella nodded, without looking up. Of course Lady Dorothy would know. She'd been aware of practically every glance happening. How embarrassing was it to know that the sexual frisson in the air every time she'd been in the same room with Oliver had probably been noticed by his mother?

Not that Lady Dorothy seemed to mind. Bella's love for her welled up and she had to look up and smile then. Lady Dorothy smiled back but her eyes were full of concern.

'There's something I should tell you before you talk to Oliver.'

'Oh?'

Lady Dorothy looked embarrassed now. 'There have always been a number of women who are interested in what Oliver has rather than who he is. It's probably contributed to how…wary he is with women.'

Bella's jaw was dropping. Surely Lady Dorothy wasn't suggesting that she was interested in Oliver's money? But Lady Dorothy held up her hand to stop her protest.

'A very long time ago, when Oliver was first at university, there was a girl who was determined to marry him. Determined enough to pretend she was pregnant.'

This time, Bella couldn't stay quiet. 'I'm not *pretending*,' she said vehemently. 'And I'm not a gold-digger. I don't want his money.' That Lady Dorothy could even suggest such a thing was astonishingly hurtful. She scrambled to her feet. 'I can take care of this baby myself. I *intend* to take care of it myself.'

'Take *care* of it?' Lady Dorothy went pale. 'You don't mean…'

Bib jumped off her lap, sensing the tension.

'No, I don't,' Bella said, not even trying to check the tears running down her cheeks. 'I *want* this baby.'

'Oh, my dear. So do I.'

Bella changed her mind about fleeing the room. She stared at Lady Dorothy.

'What I was trying to say, obviously clumsily, is that you might need to be patient with Oliver. Give him a chance?'

Bella bit her lip and scrubbed the tears from her face.

'Whatever happens between you and my son is really none of my business,' Lady Dorothy continued. 'What I will say is that I think you're a wonderful girl, Bella. You have so much love to give. So much joy that you bring to those around you. You need to know that you'll have *my* full support, financial or otherwise.'

Bella's chin rose at the repeated mention of money but Lady Dorothy shook her head. She blinked rapidly a few times and looked, horribly, as though she might be struggling with tears herself.

'You came to work for me because I reminded you of your nanna, didn't you?' she asked softly.

Bella nodded slowly.

'Well…this baby of yours will be my grandchild.' Yes, there was definitely a tremble in Lady Dorothy's voice. 'Maybe the only one I'll ever have and all I really wanted to say was that if this baby is anything like its mother, I will consider myself very blessed.'

'Oh…' It was the only word Bella was capable of. She bent down and hugged Lady Dorothy tightly.

She was still hugging her when she heard her name.

'Bella? I'd like a word, if you wouldn't mind.'

He had intended talking to Bella as soon as she'd arrived this morning but he'd mistimed it. Instead, Oliver had overheard the last thing his mother had said and what he was planning to say to Bella no longer seemed like a good idea.

How could he offer to marry her and do the best by his child when it would now seem as if he was only doing what would please his mother the most? A vaguely disquieting memory was surfacing with a vengeance now. When he'd thought that Bella was the person who had upset Lady Dorothy so much by producing the pink track pants for her to wear, he'd been prepared to go and tear strips off her to defend his mother. And he'd been embarrassed at the thought that he might seem like some kind of mummy's boy.

Offering to marry her now, after hearing those words about the impending grandchild, could very well be seen as doing exactly what his mother wanted so badly. What she might have told him to do because it was the 'right thing'.

Or, worse, simply as doing the 'right thing' because he was pompous and stuffy and…boringly predictable. The absolute opposite of everything Bella was.

By the time he'd led her into the far more formal drawing room, Oliver felt like he was back on that damned merry-go-round. The first words that burst from his mouth when he had closed the door and turned to face Bella were certainly not what he'd planned to say.

'How the *hell* did this happen, Bella?'

Bella just looked at him, her eyes huge and scared and so very, very blue. Her hair was in a loose ponytail this morning and some shorter curls had escaped to frame her face. She was breathing fast and he could see the soft skin at the top of her breasts rising and falling.

What a stupid, stupid question. He knew exactly how it had happened. And, God help him, if he had the opportunity to relive the circumstances that had caused them to be standing here like this, he would probably be unable to resist the temptation.

He'd never wanted any woman the way he *still* wanted Bella Graham.

Oliver closed his eyes, struggling for control. 'You told me you were on the Pill.'

'No. I said I was *safe*. I was talking about STDs. I'd been tested ages ago. I never slept around. I knew I—'

'I *asked* if you were on the Pill,' Oliver cut in. 'You knew you weren't and yet you let me think that the issue of an unwanted pregnancy wasn't a problem.'

'I didn't think it was. I had a morning-after pill available.'

'And you took it?'

'Of course I took it.'

There was a spark of something like real anger in Bella's eyes now. Did she think that he was suggesting she'd planned this all along, to get his name and his fortune? Well, it wouldn't be the first time and there was something in her face now that actually made him more suspicious.

Guilt. It had to be.

'*What?*' he snapped. 'What aren't you telling me, Bella?'

'It was…um…a bit past its use-by date. I didn't think it would matter.'

She was looking stricken now. A guilty child knowing she'd done something really bad.

But it was so like her, wasn't it? Slap-dash. Seizing the moment and not worrying about something that was unlikely to happen that might trip her up. Trusting her instincts, which, he had to admit, were often exactly the right things to trust.

Like the approach she'd taken with his mother. If it hadn't been for Bella's often outrageous disregard for convention and consequences, his mother might still be in a hospital bed, too depressed to consider attempting rehabilitation. Oliver would never forget the sight of those bright pink track pants stuffed into the rubbish bin. Even now, he could feel his lips wanting to curl upwards.

'I know it was irresponsible,' Bella was saying now. 'And I'm sorry.'

Oliver was sorry too. Sorry that he'd started this conversation in such an angry and negative fashion. What his mother wanted had nothing to do with this but how was Bella to know that at some point during the long and sleepless night he'd just suffered, he'd realised that he *wanted* to marry her?

That this pregnancy might be a blessing in disguise. The prod he needed to get past all the…stuffiness he'd surrounded himself with for so many years as he did the 'right thing' and avoided painful emotional involvements.

Maybe the thing that had tipped the balance was knowing that if he didn't marry her, she would disappear.

He understood now why she'd been so quiet and, OK,

well behaved in the last few weeks. She'd known about the pregnancy. Part of her had gone AWOL then and he'd been haunted by it, hadn't he? Constantly thinking about her when he was supposed to be focussed on his work. Knowing that something wasn't right.

Missing her.

If she disappeared from his life, how much worse would that feeling that something was missing become?

It would become unbearable, that's what.

Because, at a somewhat later point in the night, probably when dawn had been about to break, the pieces had fallen into place, followed by a sense of peace that had led to him finally falling deeply asleep—the reason he hadn't been upstairs and ready for Bella's arrival, as he'd intended to be.

That peace had come from knowing that the feeling that he'd always burned off with his exercise had gone and it had gone for good. That feeling that something was missing from his life and he didn't know what it was—had he really only experienced it again yesterday when he'd been watching Bella with her family?

He knew what it was now.

Not simply family, even though he knew his mother was right and he had the chance here to become a part of a *real* family. One where there was a bond between every member and not an island of protection like the bond he'd had with his mother as a child.

No. What had been missing had been the kind of love you could only have with someone who wasn't a member of your family. The kind that gave birth to a new generation. A new family.

The kind of love he had for Bella.

Now was the time to tell her. Not to do the 'right thing' but to put things right. To make them as they should be. But he had some explaining to do first, didn't he?

'We come from very different backgrounds, Bella, don't we?'

She was eyeing him warily, as if she was expecting him to accuse her of fortune hunting. Oliver gave his head an unconscious shake, denying the suspicion.

'My parents got married because it was expected of them. Not because they had ever been in love with each other.'

Bella made a soft, huffing sound. 'Are you about to tell me they got married because your mother was pregnant?'

'What? Good God, no.' The idea was just as bizarre as imagining Lady Dorothy wearing bright pink track pants with an elasticised waist. 'No. They came from the same social circle. People who shared the same aspirations and values. Everybody thought it was a perfect match.'

'And was it?'

'No. Far from it.'

'Well…there you go, then.'

'Sorry?' The comment was incomprehensible enough to fuel a gathering confusion.

What was it he'd been intending to say? Something about having told her a relationship between them was inappropriate but not because she didn't fit the expected mould of the people who'd always been in his life. The inappropriateness was because *he* wasn't the kind of man she should probably be with.

Oliver was afraid to tell her how he felt, he realised, because it was entirely possible that Bella would tell him it couldn't possibly happen. That he would be a dead weight in the kind of life she had planned for herself. That he would hold her back and make her life less exciting. Less fun.

'Expectations aren't reliable, are they?' Bella's question was crisp.

Was she referring to his parents' marriage? 'No,' Oliver agreed. 'They're not.'

Bella was standing straight and tall in front of him. Her gaze was intense. Fierce, even.

'I'm not that girl you knew at university, Oliver. I'm not after your money and I certainly don't expect you to offer to marry me.'

She drew in such a decisive breath it sounded like a sniff.

'And you can forget any expectations that you need to marry me because I'm pregnant,' she added, turning on her heel. 'We live in a very different generation from your parents, Oliver, and I wouldn't consider marrying anyone who wasn't in love with me. Or who *I* wasn't in love *with*.'

Oliver found himself left standing alone, staring after Bella as she wrenched the door open and marched through it. What had that meant?

That it wouldn't make any difference if he told her that he was in love with her?

Because she wasn't in love with *him*?

He couldn't leave things like this. Oliver strode after Bella. His mother was coming out of the conservatory and he couldn't ignore her expression.

'What's wrong?'

'I forgot that the door was open. Bib ran away into the garden and she might get lost. Bella looked terribly upset.'

Bella was probably upset about a lot more than the cat. With good reason. He'd made a complete mess of trying to talk to her, hadn't he? Oliver headed into the conservatory and towards the open French doors.

'Stay here and don't worry,' he told his mother. 'I'm going to see what I can do to fix things.'

CHAPTER THIRTEEN

IT WAS hard to see through a mist of tears.

Bella blinked hard but the part of the garden that came into focus was the rose-covered summer house and, for a heartbeat, she was lying in Oliver's arms again. Being made love to.

Being *loved*.

It would never happen again. Bella stumbled as the image was blurred by fresh tears. He'd spelt it out, hadn't he? He had been going to offer to marry her because it was the expected thing to do in his world. Maybe the reasons for the expectations for his parents to marry had been different but the result would be the same.

A far from perfect result.

But Oliver was still prepared to go through with it?

Well, she wasn't. No way.

Even if it broke Lady Dorothy's heart not to have potentially her only grandchild in the family.

Bella stopped in her tracks for a moment, gulping in the fresh, ocean-tinged air. Controlling her tears because it was stupid to go charging down the steps when she couldn't see properly. She'd end up falling and everybody knew how dangerous that was for pregnant women.

She'd told Lady Dorothy that she could take care of this baby and she could. Starting now.

'Bib?' The cat's name came out as little more than a whisper. Bella took another deep breath and cleared her throat. 'Bib? Where are you?'

Her voice was stronger now. *She* was stronger. She *could* cope. When she found Bib, she would go back to Kate and Connor's house and then she'd have time to really pull herself together and get her head around what the future held. As much as she loved Lady Dorothy, she couldn't keep working and living in the same house as Oliver. They would manage. They'd managed just fine yesterday without her.

She couldn't go home without Bib, though. Kate might have been totally against having a fur child when the kitten had arrived in their lives, but Bella knew how much she loved her pet now. Imagine coming home from a honeymoon to be told that Bib had been lost. Washed out to sea or attacked by a seagull or something.

The steps that led down the cliff to the almost private beach were steep but perfectly manageable. After about a dozen of them, Bella paused and called again and this time she heard something. A mewing sound that was definitely that of a cat but it sounded nothing like Bib. It was miserable and frightened and it struck such a chord with how Bella was feeling that her breath came out in a sob.

The sound was coming from somewhere further up the cliff but Bella couldn't see a fluffy grey shape anywhere. Cautiously, she moved away from the steps onto a natural terrace that was supporting some shrubs around the base of an old pohutukawa tree leaning out towards the sea at a precarious angle.

'Bib? Come on, kitten. Where are you?'

And then Bella could finally pinpoint where the sad cry was coming from. Bib must have raced up the trunk of the pohutukawa tree and then out onto one of the branches on the far side that hung straight out from the cliff. Maybe she'd looked down and seen the rocks on the beach far below and realised how much danger she was in.

There was no way Bella could climb up to fetch her. The only option to save Bib would be to coax her back towards the solid main trunk of the tree but that wasn't going to be easy. She could see the bottlebrush of a tail and the stiff posture of a terrified cat that wasn't going anywhere in a hurry.

The roots of the tree were a twisted nest that seemed well anchored into the cliff side. Carefully, Bella climbed over some of them. If she could get close enough to the trunk, maybe Bib would respond to her calls. The roots were certainly sturdy enough but what Bella hadn't taken account of was the dry, crumbly soil between them. Her foot went straight through what looked like a solid part of the ledge and there was only air beneath it. She lost her balance and found herself falling.

And she could hear her name being shouted.

'Bella!'

Oliver's heart stopped when he saw Bella falling. It started again with a painful thump as he leapt down the final few steps to the level of that ledge, her name wrenched out of him in an agonised cry.

The dreadful fear was contained when he saw that Bella hadn't fallen very far at all. She was caught between tree roots and was in no danger of falling to the rocks below. Instantly, the fear morphed into anger as he moved onto the ledge.

'For God's sake, Bella.' He was careful enough to keep hold of the roots above his head with one hand, close enough to reach his other hand down to where she could grasp it. He hauled her to her feet, more angry words pouring out. 'You just couldn't be bothered sticking to the steps? Not adventurous enough for you? Too predictable? Boring? What were trying to do, anyway—find a short cut down to the beach?'

He knew he shouldn't be shouting at her. He hated the way she was staring up at him, looking so terrified as he pulled her closer. But there was no way he could contain that fear and anger any longer.

'You scared the *hell* out of me,' he informed her as she got close enough for him to catch her with both hands. To pull her into his arms and back to the safety of the steps.

Bella was shaking like a leaf. And sobbing. All Oliver could do was sink down onto the wide step and hold her in his arms, cradled against his chest. He stroked her hair and asked questions that she was nowhere near ready to answer.

'What were you doing?

'Have you hurt yourself?

'Are you getting any cramps or anything?'

Eventually, he felt the shaking subside and he heard Bella take a deeper breath.

'I'm fine,' she said, in a small voice.

She'd done it again, hadn't she?

Done something stupid in front of Oliver. No wonder he was angry but why was he still holding her like this? He'd been stroking her hair even, as though he really cared about her. The stroking had stopped but Bella could feel a different kind of touch. Oliver's face pressed against her hair? It had to be because she could feel the puff of his breath on her cheek.

And when she turned her head a little, his lips were right there.

And he was *kissing* her.

Kissing her with a passion that was barely under control. A tenderness that was laced with…fear?

'I could have lost you,' Oliver murmured between kisses. 'You could have lost the baby.'

'But you don't want the baby.' Bella had to pull back far enough to see his face. 'My getting pregnant was an accident.' She screwed her eyes shut. 'No. It wasn't an accident. It was me being stupid. Like I always am.'

'No. You're not stupid, Bella. Just…impetuous.' Oliver was smiling at her. 'It's one of the things that makes us so different. One of the things I love about you so much.'

Love? Had the L word just crossed Oliver Dawson's lips?

Unbelievable. Maybe she had knocked her head without realising it.

It might be a good idea to change the subject before

she really made an idiot of herself and told him about all the things she loved about *him*.

'I was trying to rescue Bib,' she told him. 'She's out there on the branch. See?'

Oliver seemed to have difficulty changing the direction of his gaze. Bib got no more than a brief glance.

'She's safe enough for the moment. Cats are very good at getting out of trees. They just need a bit of time to figure things out.' Oliver was pressing his lips on Bella's hair now. 'Right now, it's *you* I care about. Only you.'

Bella was staying very still in his arms. She hadn't imagined it this time. If she didn't move for a while, maybe it would start seeming real.

'I was trying to tell you,' Oliver said. 'That's why I told you about my parents because I wanted you to understand that it was different for us. That I didn't want to marry you just because other people might expect it.'

'But...you said that we came from very different backgrounds.'

'And we do. Thank goodness. And maybe some people will think it's not a perfect match. Maybe that's what you think too but...I'm in love with you, Bella. So much in love.'

There it was again. The L word.

'And maybe I'm just lucky that you were careless about contraception because now there's a chance that you might consider marrying me.'

Bella was confused again. 'Why wouldn't I?'

'Because I'm...stuffy. Boring and predictable.' Oliver

was smiling again as he tightened his hold on Bella. 'Like the steps?'

'You're crazy,' she told him. A smile was trying to break out on her face. She could feel it coming, her face muscles softening. Her heart singing. 'I'd marry you if there was never going to be a baby.'

'You would?' The mix of surprise and delight in Oliver's voice made Bella's smile escape further.

'Of course I would. I love you, Oliver. I have for ages. Ever since you smiled at me that time. That first day when I was looking after your mother.'

For a long, long moment, they simply gazed at each other. Basking in the kind of glow that only newly declared love could bring.

The gift of that love was the biggest joy that Bella had ever received. She wanted to do something just as big for Oliver.

'I promise I won't do anything irresponsible again,' she whispered.

Oliver simply smiled. 'You are who you are, Bella, and I love you. Maybe my stuffiness will help keep you safe in the future. You will certainly keep reminding me how joyful life can be. What it feels like to be *really* alive.'

Bella's smile couldn't get any bigger. She could never feel any happier. This moment was absolutely perfect. Except…

Except poor Bib was still stuck in the tree.

Bella tore her gaze from that of the man who was going to become her husband and looked over her shoulder, up into the branches of the old tree. As she did so, she could hear the faint cry of an elderly woman's voice coming from the garden well above the step she was sitting on with Oliver.

'Bib? Bib, Bib, Bib? Come here at once, you naughty cat.'

Bella wasn't the only one who'd heard the command. Oliver was smiling. And Bib? The small, fluffy grey and white cat trotted along the thin branch until it got to the main trunk of the tree. Then she turned herself around and shimmied down backwards until she reached ground level. With barely a glance at the couple locked in each other's arms, Bib scooted past, up the steps, towards the garden and Lady Dorothy.

Bella laughed. 'She knows who she wants to get a cuddle from.'

'So do I.' Oliver's arms tightened around Bella again.

She raised her face for another kiss but a tiny frown was creasing Oliver's brow.

'What about all the things you were dreaming of for your future, my love?'

'Like what?'

'A dozen kids?'

Bella grinned. 'It's a big house. We could fit in more than one, couldn't we?'

Oliver laughed but then looked serious again.

'The overseas travel?'

'Aren't we going to have a honeymoon?'

'Of course. We could go anywhere you want. Where would you most want to go?'

'Ooh…London,' Bella said dreamily. 'Barcelona. Paris.' She kissed Oliver. 'We could go dancing in Paris.'

Oliver made a face. 'They do line dancing in Paris?'

Bella shook her head, laughing. 'Tango,' she told him. 'That's the only dance for Paris, I think. I'll teach you.'

It was Oliver's turn to kiss her. 'It takes two to tango,' he whispered.

'Lucky we've got each other, then, isn't it?' Bella wanted to hold this moment for ever. To look into Oliver's gorgeous brown eyes. To have him looking at her like this. With so much love. 'There's two of us.'

Oliver's gaze softened even more. 'And there always will be,' he said softly. 'Always.'

CHAPTER FOURTEEN

THE Dawson wedding was a much more lavish affair than Kate and Connor's wedding had been.

It was held in one of the most prestigious churches the city of Auckland had to offer and the guest list ran to hundreds.

The guest with the prime position in the front row was, of course, Lady Dorothy Dawson. For this wedding she was wearing another silk dress and matching jacket and hat but this time they were in shades of apricot and they were an even better match for the garnet necklace she had chosen for her accessory.

And this time she was wearing her matching ring—a symbol of just how far she had come in her recovery.

Sitting beside her, Kate was glowing with her advancing pregnancy and Connor already had the air of a proud father. Thanks to the most recent scan, he knew he would be welcoming a son into the world before very long. Bella had had a scan at almost the same time but she and Oliver had decided to keep the gender of their baby a secret. The knowledge that there would be two little boys so close in age keeping the family bonds strong was a treasure they weren't quite ready to share.

Bella's dress wasn't as slim fitting as Kate's had been

but there was still no hiding the bump of her expanding belly. And, yes, there'd been a few sideways glances from some of the Dawson social set who would have been terribly offended if they hadn't been invited to the wedding of the year but it didn't bother Oliver or Bella or Lady Dorothy one little bit.

They'd made the wedding arrangements with all the speed possible for such an occasion because it was very important that Oliver and Bella could have their honeymoon before the pregnancy made it impossible to embark on an international flight.

Before their family responsibilities made it impossible to spend a night dancing a tango in Paris.

A dance for two people.

A dance of love.

* * * * *

ROMANCE

The Secrets She Carried	Lynne Graham
To Love, Honour and Betray	Jennie Lucas
Heart of a Desert Warrior	Lucy Monroe
Unnoticed and Untouched	Lynn Raye Harris
A Royal World Apart	Maisey Yates
Distracted by her Virtue	Maggie Cox
The Count's Prize	Christina Hollis
The Tarnished Jewel of Jazaar	Susanna Carr
Keeping Her Up All Night	Anna Cleary
The Rules of Engagement	Ally Blake
Argentinian in the Outback	Margaret Way
The Sheriff's Doorstep Baby	Teresa Carpenter
The Sheikh's Jewel	Melissa James
The Rebel Rancher	Donna Alward
Always the Best Man	Fiona Harper
How the Playboy Got Serious	Shirley Jump
Sydney Harbour Hospital: Marco's Temptation	Fiona McArthur
Dr Tall, Dark...and Dangerous?	Lynne Marshall

MEDICAL

The Legendary Playboy Surgeon	Alison Roberts
Falling for Her Impossible Boss	Alison Roberts
Letting Go With Dr Rodriguez	Fiona Lowe
Waking Up With His Runaway Bride	Louisa George

Mills & Boon® Large Print

July 2012

ROMANCE

Roccanti's Marriage Revenge — Lynne Graham
The Devil and Miss Jones — Kate Walker
Sheikh Without a Heart — Sandra Marton
Savas's Wildcat — Anne McAllister
A Bride for the Island Prince — Rebecca Winters
The Nanny and the Boss's Twins — Barbara McMahon
Once a Cowboy... — Patricia Thayer
When Chocolate Is Not Enough... — Nina Harrington

HISTORICAL

The Mysterious Lord Marlowe — Anne Herries
Marrying the Royal Marine — Carla Kelly
A Most Unladylike Adventure — Elizabeth Beacon
Seduced by Her Highland Warrior — Michelle Willingham

MEDICAL

The Boss She Can't Resist — Lucy Clark
Heart Surgeon, Hero...Husband? — Susan Carlisle
Dr Langley: Protector or Playboy? — Joanna Neil
Daredevil and Dr Kate — Leah Martyn
Spring Proposal in Swallowbrook — Abigail Gordon
Doctor's Guide to Dating in the Jungle — Tina Beckett

0612 GEN STD LP

Mills & Boon® Hardback

August 2012

ROMANCE

Contract with Consequences	Miranda Lee
The Sheikh's Last Gamble	Trish Morey
The Man She Shouldn't Crave	Lucy Ellis
The Girl He'd Overlooked	Cathy Williams
A Tainted Beauty	Sharon Kendrick
One Night With The Enemy	Abby Green
The Dangerous Jacob Wilde	Sandra Marton
His Last Chance at Redemption	Michelle Conder
The Hidden Heart of Rico Rossi	Kate Hardy
Marrying the Enemy	Nicola Marsh
Mr Right, Next Door!	Barbara Wallace
The Cowboy Comes Home	Patricia Thayer
The Rancher's Housekeeper	Rebecca Winters
Her Outback Rescuer	Marion Lennox
Monsoon Wedding Fever	Shoma Narayanan
If the Ring Fits...	Jackie Braun
Sydney Harbour Hospital: Ava's Re-Awakening	Carol Marinelli
How To Mend A Broken Heart	Amy Andrews

MEDICAL

Falling for Dr Fearless	Lucy Clark
The Nurse He Shouldn't Notice	Susan Carlisle
Every Boy's Dream Dad	Sue MacKay
Return of the Rebel Surgeon	Connie Cox

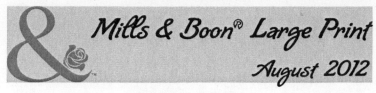
Mills & Boon® Large Print
August 2012

ROMANCE

A Deal at the Altar	Lynne Graham
Return of the Moralis Wife	Jacqueline Baird
Gianni's Pride	Kim Lawrence
Undone by His Touch	Annie West
The Cattle King's Bride	Margaret Way
New York's Finest Rebel	Trish Wylie
The Man Who Saw Her Beauty	Michelle Douglas
The Last Real Cowboy	Donna Alward
The Legend of de Marco	Abby Green
Stepping out of the Shadows	Robyn Donald
Deserving of His Diamonds?	Melanie Milburne

HISTORICAL

The Scandalous Lord Lanchester	Anne Herries
Highland Rogue, London Miss	Margaret Moore
His Compromised Countess	Deborah Hale
The Dragon and the Pearl	Jeannie Lin
Destitute On His Doorstep	Helen Dickson

MEDICAL

Sydney Harbour Hospital: Lily's Scandal	Marion Lennox
Sydney Harbour Hospital: Zoe's Baby	Alison Roberts
Gina's Little Secret	Jennifer Taylor
Taming the Lone Doc's Heart	Lucy Clark
The Runaway Nurse	Dianne Drake
The Baby Who Saved Dr Cynical	Connie Cox

0712 GEN STD LP